"Tell me your name, Mary Smith."

"I never said it was Smith."

"Yeah, I know. Mary, you said, from here and there. Mary Smith from Peoria works well, don't you think?"

How did he know? No one else had guessed she was lying.

He was a *giant,* she thought. There was something exciting about a man so large— something primitive and reassuring. A man like this could defend a woman against a criminal looking for the one person who could link him to three murders.

On the other hand, he might easily be henchman material, hired to seek out that same witness. The thought sent fear down her spine.

"Who are you?" she breathed.

He leaned in close. His gaze touched her mouth, lingered there. Then he drawled, "Every man your mama ever warned you about."

Dear Reader,

Welcome to another month of fine reading from Silhouette Intimate Moments. And what better way to start off the month than with an American Hero title from Marilyn Pappano, a book that's also the beginning of a new miniseries, Southern Knights. Hero Michael Bennett and his friends Remy and Smith are all dedicated to upholding the law—and to loving the right lady. And in *Michael's Gift*, she turns out to be the one woman he wishes she wasn't. To know more, you'll just have to read this terrific story.

The month continues with *Snow Bride*, the newest from bestselling writer Dallas Schulze. Then it's on to *Wild Horses, Wild Men*, from Ann Williams; *Waking Nightmare*, from highly regarded newcomer Alicia Scott; *Breaking the Rules*, Ruth Wind's Intimate Moments debut; and *Hear No Evil*, a suspenseful novel from brand-new author Susan Drake. I think you'll enjoy each and every one of these books—and that you'll be looking for more equally exciting reading next month and in the months to come. So look no further than Silhouette Intimate Moments, where, each and every month, we're proud to bring you writers we consider among the finest in the genre today.

Enjoy!

Leslie J. Wainger
Senior Editor and Editorial Coordinator

Please address questions and book requests to:
Silhouette Reader Service
U.S.: 3010 Walden Ave., P.O. Box 1325, Buffalo, NY 14269
Canadian: P.O. Box 609, Fort Erie, Ont. L2A 5X3

BREAKING THE RULES

Ruth Wind

Silhouette®
INTIMATE™MOMENTS®

Published by Silhouette Books

America's Publisher of Contemporary Romance

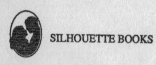 SILHOUETTE BOOKS

ISBN 0-373-07587-1

BREAKING THE RULES

Copyright © 1994 by Barbara Samuel

This edition published by arrangement with Harlequin Enterprises B. V.

Printed in U.S.A.

RUTH WIND

is the award-winning author of both contemporary and historical romance novels. She lives in the mountain Southwest with her husband, two growing sons and many animals in a hundred-year-old house the town blacksmith built. The only hobby she has since she started writing is tending the ancient garden of irises, lilies and lavender beyond her office window, and she says she can think of no more satisfying way to spend a life than growing children, books and flowers.

To Jaye Manus, a.k.a. Sherrill Lynn,
with many thanks for plotting help,
hand-holding and utterly unshakable
good sense.

And to the good Dr. House,
dentist extraordinaire,
who made it possible for me
to finish this book on time.

Prologue

She drove all night. Fast and hard through the emptiness of the Kansas plains, dotted with silos and water towers silhouetted against the clear, starry sky. In Emporia, she clutched her coat around herself and bought a cup of coffee and filled the gas tank.

By morning, she reached Pueblo. Leaving the technically stolen car in the parking lot of a huge discount store where it would eventually attract notice, she fastened her coat around her again and went inside the store. She bought a pair of soft desert boots, jeans and a handful of T-shirts, trying to ignore the collection of stares she received over her wild and incongruous appearance.

From the discount store, she crossed the street on foot to a convenience store that sold gas and food. In the bathroom there, she ripped the tags off the new things and threw her tattered dress in the waste bin. For a moment, she stared at the royal blue taffeta, bloodstained on the side and at the hem. A wave of dizzy nausea washed through her.

Once changed, she assessed herself in the fly-specked mirror. This was the hard part. With trembling hands, she braided her hip-length hair, secured it at the top and bottom, then lifted the shears she'd bought with the jeans.

"Do it, Mattie," she said to the white-faced woman in the mirror. She did, but resolve and necessity didn't keep her from weeping as she did so. Her pride and joy. Her hair.

When it was done, she held the three-foot braid in her hand, then looked at herself. The cut was ragged, but not bad, considering. With surprise, she touched her neck and shoulders.

Taking a deep breath, she coiled the braid and nestled it into her bag. No one would recognize her now. No one.

She left the car with its Kansas plates in the sprawling parking lot and hopped on a city bus that took her downtown. At the Greyhound station, she scanned the lists of destinations and impulsively bought a ticket for a little town she'd never heard of because she liked the name.

Kismet, Arizona.

They would never find her there.

Chapter 1

In the middle of the morning bustle, with country music playing in the kitchen of the café, and coffee perking and the noise of a dozen men buzzing around the room, Mattie realized that somehow or other, the job she'd taken out of desperation three weeks before was one she had learned to like. No, love.

"Order up!" called the cook. Mattie grabbed the thick porcelain plates filled with greasy eggs and strips of bacon and good white toast. Piling them on her arms, she hurried toward the table of roadworkers who would gulp the food down and tip her a dollar, no matter how well or poorly she did her job, as long as she kept their coffee cups filled. Bustling back toward the counter, she grabbed the coffeepot and swung through in a circle, touching up every cup along the route, except Joe Harriday's, who liked to get all the way to the bottom before he started again.

There was a buzz in her muscles and heat in her chest. Her hair fell in her eyes and she brushed it back, feeling the pleasant grime of hard work on her skin.

Loved it.

As the breakfast crowd thinned, leaving behind only a single pair of tourists who'd wandered in off the highway, Mattie made a fresh pot of coffee, mainly for the crew to drink as they cleaned up breakfast and got ready for lunch.

"A woman after my own heart," said Roxanne, the other waitress, breathing deeply of the scented steam rising from the pot. "You want to take a break first?"

"Go ahead, Roxanne. I can wait awhile."

"Thanks." She touched her stomach. "I'm starving."

The low, precise grumbling of a motorcycle cut through the post-rush quiet. Mattie turned to watch a bike roar up in front of the café. Through the plate-glass windows, the waitresses watched as a man parked a sleek, midnight blue machine. Chrome shone all over it. The man driving settled it easily and limberly dismounted.

Mattie stared, a prickling in her nerves.

For a minute, he stood beside the bike, looking out toward the canyon. She'd learned the hard way to be careful about men, careful about even looking too hard at one for fear she might start to want again what she couldn't have.

But it was impossible not to stare. Standing there against the backdrop of rough red sandstone cliffs and thick ponderosa pine, he looked like one of the outlaws that had hidden in the canyon long ago. Or maybe, Mattie thought, he was more like the eagles she sometimes saw on her dawn trips to the canyon—

there was in his stance the same wary alertness; in his size she felt the same sense of leashed power.

He wore a plain white cotton shirt, the long sleeves rolled to the elbows, tucked at the narrow waist into a pair of jeans. His hair, the color of coffee and tangled from his ride in the wind, was long. Very long. Casually, he finger-combed it away from his face and headed for the restaurant.

Roxanne made a low, approving sound in her throat.

The bell rang over the door and the man came in, his walk graceful and controlled. He glanced around the room, making a clean sweep, and Mattie was sure those eyes missed nothing. After the initial scope, the pale gaze swiveled back and settled on Mattie.

Mattie told herself she ought to do something with the bar towel in her hand, and managed to swipe it nervously over the counter, but she found it nearly impossible not to look up again—as if he carried with him some secret magnetic force. Even the old lady in the corner had paused with her hand on the sugar bowl, to stare.

The face was hard, made of planes carved into high, sharp arches of cheekbone, a powerful nose and harsh, clean jaw. The eyes—maybe it was his eyes—were a pale green, like water in the forest, and the color was all the more startling in contrast to the deeply suntanned skin.

When Mattie finally realized she was gaping like a child in the presence of a star quarterback, she realized he was staring at her. No smile or softness of expression marred the implacable planes of that face. Mattie shifted, but found it hard to look away.

"Hey, Zeke," Roxanne said with a purr. "Don't stand there letting the flies in. Come on in."

He settled on a stool. "Hi," he said to Mattie. "Don't believe I've seen you around here before."

The voice matched the face, for it was deep and rough as a midnight canyon, the words drawl-thickened with the sound of the South. Louisiana, at least—maybe even Mississippi.

She gathered her breath and her defenses. "No, you haven't," she said, and was pleased at the cool, even sound of her voice.

"What's your name?"

"Mary." She shifted uncomfortably and crossed her arms.

His gaze moved over her face, lingered on her mouth, slipped up to her eyes again.

"Who's gonna wait on me this morning?"

Roxanne nudged Mattie with a sideways grin. "He thinks we're going to fight over the privilege." To the man, she said, "Mary'll take care of you. I'm going on break."

The wary expression on his face eased ever so slightly as he winked at Roxanne. "My heart is broken, baby."

Mattie quelled an impulse to roll her eyes. It was obvious he thought he was the Lord's gift to women—and while that same Lord had done a fine job of packaging, she wouldn't argue with that—arrogant men of this sort were not her style. "Don't let me interfere," she said wryly. "I'll take my break."

Roxanne shook her head. "He won't bite," she said, scribbling on a ticket for her breakfast order. "And I'm famished." She ducked into the kitchen. Mattie heard her call out her order to the cook.

The man at the counter lazily pulled a pack of cigarettes from his pocket. "Guess you're stuck with me."

"What can I get you?"

"Coffee. Please."

Mattie could feel his gaze as she took a heavy white mug from the rack, settled it before him and poured coffee. "Would you like cream?" she asked formally.

He shook his head.

Lifting the pot, she inclined her head. "You know, in most places, it's considered rude to stare."

He moistened his lips and drew on the cigarette. "Is that right?"

She lowered her eyes. In the brief pause, she felt within her a strange psychic disturbance. A warning, like the shriek of a blue jay when a cat wanders by: *Danger! Danger! Danger!*

"Where you from, Mary?" he asked.

Mattie turned to precisely place the coffeepot on the burner. "Here and there," she said with a shrug. Nervously, she smoothed a wisp of hair from her face. "Do you want to look at a menu?"

He took his time pouring sugar into his cup. "No, I know what I want." Slowly, he stirred. Even such a small act rippled the rounds of muscle in his arms, and at the collar of his shirt she could see the chest, too, was powerfully muscled.

He was deeply tanned. Probably, she thought disdainfully, some body-builder type that hung out in gyms striking poses.

The light green eyes accepted and deflected her examination—and made her revise that last conclusion. No way this man played pretty boy for anyone. Maybe he'd been born well endowed or his work gave him muscles, but she knew without doubt that he didn't spend time on weight machines to satisfy any vanity on his part.

"Sir?" she prompted. "Would you like to order?"

"Sir?" he echoed ironically. "Call me Zeke." He grinned at her. "I'm not that old yet."

The grin was her undoing. His mouth was wide with full, rich lips, and he had good teeth, though a trifle crooked. But that grin was full of knowledge, full of all the things Mattie had wondered about and wanted to learn in that secret, dark part of herself.

She knocked over a ketchup bottle.

He caught it with a deft movement. In his gaze, amusement danced. "Don't get all flustered, now, Miss Mary."

"Don't flatter yourself."

"No, ma'am." The grin lingered at the edges of that fine mouth. He sipped his coffee. "Get me a couple eggs, over easy, some toast and bacon and hash browns."

Relieved, Mattie scribbled down the order, slapped it to the ring and spun it around, then escaped into the kitchen.

Zeke smoked and drank coffee idly, waiting for his food. A newspaper sat on the counter, but he didn't pick it up.

Through the open door to the kitchen, he watched the waitress collecting plates from the dish machine. He'd been on one of his periodic restless road trips the past few weeks—this one down to the Gulf for the hell of it, and the new waitress had been hired in his absence. Not from around here, but he'd swear he knew her from somewhere.

She was hiding something, that much was sure. His eyes narrowed. Mary. If he asked her last name, she'd probably say Smith. Mary Smith from Peoria.

And he was John Doe.

He watched her as she put the plates away. A nice-looking woman if you liked the type, which he ordinarily didn't. He preferred blondes, generally. Tall blondes, with lean bodies and hard eyes. This one was smaller, with tawny skin and dark hair. She tried to hide her figure under the loose-fitting uniform, but the curves were a tad too generous to be well hidden. Round breasts and naturally swaying hips. Her hair was short, but thick and silky-looking and he couldn't help but admire the graceful turn of her neck above the white collar.

Nice-looking, with the emphasis on the nice. Probably Catholic school and the whole nine yards; a woman didn't keep skin like that living hard.

Which meant she wasn't someone he'd tangled with and forgotten. Zeke didn't bother with good girls, sweet girls like this one. They were looking for things he just didn't ever intend to provide for anyone.

He continued to watch her through the door to the kitchen. For a good girl, she sure had one hell of a mouth. Generous, with plump lips and a certain slanting curve at the corners that hinted the doe eyes might light with mischief when she wasn't scared.

Maybe that's what he remembered—a kissable mouth was his particular downfall, as he'd told himself more than once.

He wondered what a good girl had to hide, what she was running from.

And swore. A pretty mouth and a woman in trouble. Bad combination, especially on some sweet stranger he don't know a damned thing about. An alarm bell triggered in his mind.

It would come to him. He'd figure out where he knew her from. In the meantime, he had troubles of his own.

The cook smacked a bell and slid Zeke's order under the heat lamp. Mary wiped her palms on her apron and headed out to pick it up. Zeke caught her nervous glance in his direction, and taking the chance, frankly watched her breasts move under her blouse. It would irritate her. Push her away.

She pretended not to notice, but he could see by the flush in her cheeks that she had. "Would you like anything else to go with that?" she asked, slamming the thick plate down in front of him.

He looked at her. Big, big brown eyes, snapping now with both desire and fury. The unwilling desire sent a spiral of response through his nether regions, and he almost taunted her, just to see if he could kindle that flame a little bit. He almost said, "Yeah, I want you, nothing on it."

But along with the desire and wariness in those enormous brown eyes, he saw innocence. It was one thing to play with a woman who understood the stakes, who didn't expect a man to call back in the morning. Zeke had rules about virgins and innocents. "That'll be it," he said. "Thanks."

She slapped the check on the counter and automatically refilled his coffee cup. Zeke pretended to ignore her, but as she turned back toward the coffee machine, he spied her hands. Burns. It triggered another sense of déjà vu. He frowned. "Mary. Where do I know you from?"

Her face went abruptly, sickeningly white. "You must have somebody else in mind," she said, and hurried away.

Zeke felt a sinking sensation in the pit of his stomach. She was lying. And she was in trouble. Mary Smith from Peoria.

Right.

In the kitchen, over the roar of the dishwasher, Roxanne met Mattie. "Figures," Roxanne said matter-of-factly. "I've been trying to catch Zeke Shephard's eye since he showed up in Kismet. He walks in and takes one look at you and it's fire." She leaned over and sniffed Mattie's neck. "Nope. No perfume."

Mattie slapped her arm. "Just tell him if you want him. He doesn't look like the type who'd say no." She looked at Roxanne. Long blond hair and a lean body, with big blue eyes. "I can't see too many men that would say no to you, anyway."

Roxanne grinned. "Thanks." She folded her arms across her chest and glanced out the kitchen door. "He wouldn't say no, but I couldn't catch him like that, either."

"Catch him?"

"Yeah." She lifted a shoulder with a coquettish smile. "One taste would never be enough. I'd want to hang on to him—at least for a little while. The woman that can tame him permanently probably hasn't been born, but he could be coaxed to light for a few months, maybe."

Mattie stared at her. In her other life, the women didn't talk about taming men. They talked about engagement rings and weddings and finding a house. She licked her lips, curious. "Wouldn't you fall in love?"

Roxanne nodded with a slight, one shouldered shrug. "Probably."

"So how could you just sleep with him, knowing he would leave you?"

"Oh, honey. I pegged you for naive, but I didn't think you were stupid." Roxanne tugged Mattie's sleeve, pulling her over to look out the door to where Zeke sat, eating heartily. Against the backlight of the window, his hair gleamed around the edges with a deep, burnished halo. In a low voice, Roxanne said, "I want you to think about that man in your bed, with nothing on except maybe a sheet."

Mattie shot her an alarmed glance.

Roxanne smiled. "Just try it."

Slowly, Mattie turned to look at him. Her heart shimmered in anticipation, a strange danger, but the old ways of living had landed her in more trouble than she could fathom. Maybe Roxanne was right.

She inclined her head and let her eyes wash over the broad shoulders and lean waist, and she called up a picture—his arms bare, with that hair tangling over his shoulders, his skin dark against the white sheet.

"You see?" Roxanne said quietly. "It would be worth it."

He blotted his lips with a paper napkin, and Mattie noticed his hands were as enormous as the rest of him. For one single minute, she indulged in her first experience with pure lust and let herself imagine what that hand might feel like, gliding over her body.

As if he felt her gaze, he looked up suddenly. Caught in the forbidden thoughts, Mattie didn't immediately look away. He met her gaze levelly, without emotion, acknowledging her stare without revealing anything of his own. His lips pursed as if in thought and still Mattie couldn't stop staring.

He winked and blew her a kiss.

Mortified, she turned around and ran into Roxanne's shoulder. "Oh, I'm so embarrassed," she said, covering her eyes. "What a jerk."

Roxanne laughed. "He's cocky, all right. But that's part of the game."

A wisp of her heated imaginings brushed through her. Mattie shifted uncomfortably. "That's not a game I want to play."

"Too late, honey," Roxanne said with a slow smile. "You already made the first move."

Chapter 2

Zeke kept a room above Bronco's, Kismet's premier beer/pool hall/hamburger joint, where he sometimes worked when he was in town. He stopped in to check his mail. None, which he'd expected. One side effect of cutting ties was a drop in mail. Whistling, he tossed his duffel on the bed, took a fishing pole from the closet and headed out.

Fishing calmed him. Always had. He liked everything about it: the quiet and the solitude, the play of sunlight on the water and through the trees, the smell of leaf mold beneath his feet and the faintly coppery scent of the stream. Kismet boasted some fine fishing, too. Only place there was better trout was on his land in Colorado, and he hadn't been there in some time.

This morning, however, the gentle scenery only provided a backdrop for the nagging sense of déjà vu he'd felt over the new waitress at the café. No matter how he struggled with it, he couldn't place just where he knew her from, and it was driving him crazy. A cynical, suspicious part of his mind wondered if she were some friend of Amanda's come to mete out more revenge.

But that scenario didn't quite wash. For one thing, she was scared. She'd gone so pale so fast when he asked her how he knew her, Zeke had thought she might really faint.

For another thing, she pricked his instincts. It had been a long time since he'd felt that scream along his nerves.

Leave it alone, he told himself. Stay away from her, let her solve her own problems.

Leave it alone.

But as he reeled in a nice string of rainbows, he found himself wondering over and over again why he thought he knew her. It might be something as simple as he'd seen her at some rodeo, but somehow, that didn't ring quite right. He knew there was more to it than that.

The rainbows he took back to the bar, intending to hand them over to the boss, Ed, who would put them to good use.

The bartender, Sue, children in tow, was in to pick up her check. She looked as strained as she had when he'd left on his most recent road trip. "James still not working?" he asked, giving her shoulder a squeeze.

"He found some temporary construction work down in Tucson," she said, shifting the baby on her hip. "It's just hard when he's gone." She gestured ruefully to the children. "I'm worn out."

The baby gurgled, reaching a chubby hand for Zeke and giving him a grin. "Hey, little bit," he said, taking the baby. "You got yourself some teeth since last time, didn't you?"

"Getting some more, too," Sue said with a sigh. "He's been so cranky."

The baby grabbed Zeke's thumb and tried to gnaw on it. "That's nasty, sweet pea." He tickled him to distract him and said to Sue, "I just caught a nice string of fish. Why don't you bring the boys over later on and I'll fry it up. Give you a little break before work."

Sue smiled, and the expression eased some of the exhaustion around her eyes. "That would be very nice, Zeke. I've got to work at seven, so about five, I guess?"

"Who's keeping the children?"

She smiled. "Is that a hint?"

"Yes, ma'am." Zeke kissed the baby's head and gave the two-year-old a wink.

The new waitress at the cafe flitted through his mind again. "Sue, have you met the new woman at the diner?"

"Mary? Sure. She's been here three or four weeks. Seems nice enough." Sue lifted an eyebrow. "Can it be the lone wolf might actually be interested in a woman?"

Zeke shook his head. "Nothing like that." He frowned. "What's her story?"

"I don't know. She seems kind of skittish, doesn't she?"

Zeke nodded. "Yeah, exactly."

But he promised himself he'd leave it alone.

Mattie got off work at two, and changed before heading to the grocery store. As she ambled toward the small place she had rented, her limbs tingled with the hard work of her day. Her purse was heavy with tips—Roxanne cashed hers in every day, but Mattie liked the stacks of silver quarters. She rolled them up every third day. The woman at the grocery store, which doubled as a bait shop, had taken to teasing her about it.

Kismet was not exactly a town. There was the Greyhound station and café, the bait shop and grocery store. A gas station served the tourists on their way to Oak Creek Canyon. Two liquor stores and a single bar completed the picture.

Which was why Zeke Shephard came as such a shock. How could she have missed a man like that?

She hadn't. In spite of his insistence that he knew her from somewhere, there was no way Mattie had ever seen that face before.

The cabin she had rented was one of a series in a motel. The owner, seeing she planned to stay on awhile, had cut her a deal, charging her monthly instead of weekly for the quaint little place. Located a half mile from the café through gently rising pine forest and the red stones that eventually formed the famous Oak Creek Canyon, it was the most peaceful place she'd ever seen. No television or radio, but a tiny kitchenette and a sofa shoved beneath the window met her living needs.

She waved to the owner as she passed the office. He grinned and waved back. Business was good today, she noted, counting the cars lined up before the discreetly scattered but plentiful cabins.

Hers was on the end, hidden away in the pines and ferns. Feeling a rich sense of well-being, she shifted her small cache of supplies to her right hip and scrambled in her purse for her keys. She ducked under a tree.

The motorcycle was parked in the place she'd have put a car if she owned one. Amid the silence and quiet greenery of nature, it was almost leeringly modern. All that chrome and the long handlebars and midnight blue tank.

Her stomach swooped and she froze, looking around for the owner of that dangerous machine. He sat on her small concrete porch, leaning against her screen door. One long, long leg was kicked out before him, the other bent so he could rest his forearm on his knee, and his shirt pulled tight over the muscles of chest and shoulders. On his face was a pair of mirrored sunglasses.

Mattie clutched her groceries and contemplated running away. The little game she'd played earlier with Roxanne in the restaurant now seemed hopelessly juvenile and embarrassing.

"What do you want?" she asked flatly.

For a long moment, he said nothing at all. Then he stood up and took off the glasses. He sighed and looked at her regretfully. "I want to figure out where I know you from."

She'd been half expecting some sexy parry. Terror licked her lungs, as cold as dry ice, as cold as his hard face and direct eyes. "I don't know."

"Mmm." He inclined his head and his hip jutted out to one side as he hooked a thumb in the belt loop of his jeans. "Then maybe you could tell me what it is you're running from."

How did he know?

It was too much. Mattie felt her arms go weak with rubbery fear. She felt her hold loosening on the bag she held, but helplessly watched as it slipped from her grip and fell to the ground.

The brown paper bag exploded on impact, scattering her supplies over the grass at her feet. She didn't move immediately to pick them up; didn't think her arms would follow the command.

Zeke just stood there, looking at her impassively, a lock of his wild long hair lifting on a finger of wind. "You dropped somethin'."

She glanced down. Celery and apples and nuts nestled in the grass. A bottle of soda water came to rest against a bright blue box of tampons. Naturally. If you had to drop your groceries in front of some strange man, there was bound to be either tampons or PMS medicine in the mix. Murphy's Law.

Nothing had to be gathered instantly. Mattie planted her hands on her hips. "I want you to leave. Now."

"You know, Miss Mary, you can let me figure it out on my own, or you can tell me yourself."

"Go away," she said, shoving her bangs from her face.

He shifted. For a minute, Mattie thought he was going to listen to her. That he was going to swing those long legs over the saddle of his bike and ride away.

He crossed the small space between them and knelt in the grass. "Let me help you."

"I don't want your help. I want you to leave."

"I know," he said amiably, gathering loose apples into his long-fingered hands. "But I'm not going to just yet, so you may as well let me help you."

Mattie stared at the crown of his head, looking at the fall of his hair over his shoulders. The main color was a glossy shade of pecan, but the sun had coaxed lighter strands through it, and it had the kind of texture that half curled, half waved, giving it a look of disarray. She touched her bare neck, remembering the feel of hair sweeping over her neck with an acute sense of loss.

At her feet, Zeke grabbed the box of tampons. "You'll have to get the rest," he said, and headed for the front door.

Hastily, she gathered the few items remaining. "Just drop it all on the porch," she said. "I'll take everything in."

"That's all right," he said with a lazy smile. "I don't mind."

She narrowed her eyes. "That sexy Southern boy routine isn't gonna work with me," she said.

"No?" His grin—that devilish, knowing grin—said he thought otherwise.

"Put my things down and get out of here."

The bantering, lazy attitude disappeared instantly, as if it were a clear invisible shell he donned and dropped at will. Now the other man came through. Hard eyes that saw too much, a certain dangerous aura she couldn't pinpoint exactly, but was as visible as his long hair. Through the thin white cotton of his shirt, she saw one shoulder bore a dark mark—a tattoo of some kind.

He scared the hell out of her, but she'd been through a lot. A lot worse than some dangerous, sexy stranger standing on her porch holding spilled groceries.

"Tell me your name, Mary Smith."

"I never said it was Smith."

"Yeah, I know. Mary, you said, from here and there. Mary Smith from Peoria works pretty well, don't you think?" Again he lifted those ironic, suspicious eyebrows. "As well as anything else."

How did he know? she asked herself again. No one else had guessed she was lying. To cover the trembling in her arms, she marched toward him, key in hand. She had to pass him to get to the door and he didn't move much out of her way. It was an obnoxious maneuver. She elbowed him sideways, trying to keep the ripple of awareness from overtaking her senses.

But damn, she thought as she fumbled with the stupid key, in addition to that aura of sex appeal he wore like exotic cologne, he was a *giant*. Her head didn't even reach his shoulder. There was something exciting about a man so large—something primitive and reassuring that probably went back to caveman days. A big man like this might have a chance of defending a woman.

On the other hand, he might very easily be henchman material, hired to seek out that very same witness. The thought sent fingers of icy fear over her spine.

The key slipped home. Mattie opened the door and dumped her armful of groceries on a small table, then went to take Zeke's load from him. He stood on her porch, as if sensing she didn't want him to cross the threshold.

She plucked the groceries from his brawny arms and he stood there, cloaked in an amused calm, allowing her to take them, his gaze following her movements with a concentrated attention Mattie felt as a caress on her body. She felt him notice her legs, her hips, her breasts. It was not entirely unpleasant.

The last item he held was an apple. He held it up. "You know about apples, don't you?" he said lazily, and bit into it with his strong white teeth. The flesh made a sharp cracking noise and a little of the juice moistened his lower lip.

A jolt of pure desire blazed through Mattie's chest. Who would have dreamed an apple could be such a sexy thing?

He watched her, his gaze glimmering with something hot and promising. Mattie, halted a few inches from him, was struck deeply by two things.

The first was his scent. Not cologne or soap or anything artificial, it was deep and elemental, like moist earth steaming in the sun of a summer noon. And with the scent came a sense of heat, as if he were fevered.

The combination was so alluring, Mattie forgot to be careful, forgot she had to be on guard against everyone. She found herself, once again, simply staring at him, snared by the hard planes and generous mouth and unusual pale green eyes. The elusive shimmer made the color seem to flicker oddly, and Mattie felt another bolt of bone-deep yearning.

"Who are you?" she breathed.

He leaned in close. His gaze touched her mouth, lingered there. "Every man your mama ever warned you about," he said softly, the drawl slipping through her flesh like an incantation.

That brought her around. What an arrogant pig! "I don't have a mother, and I think you watch too many bad movies if you have to resort to lines like that."

One arched dark eyebrow lifted. "Yeah?" Bracing himself on the threshold with one hand, the apple in the other, Zeke swayed toward Mattie until that rich, sensual mouth hung suspended just millimeters from her own. His breath whispered over her lips as he spoke. "You keep lookin' at me like that and it'll be more than secrets that I get from that pretty mouth of yours."

She just looked at him, amazed and stunned that, after so many years, she could feel the kind of arousal she felt now, over a man she'd never seen twelve hours before.

He went still. Very, very still. With one finger, he lightly stroked her bottom lip. Stunned by the narcotic effect he had on her, Mattie allowed the slow deliberate touch.

Abruptly, he pulled away. His lips turned up in something very close to a sneer. "I'm not playing this game, Miss Mary."

Stung, she hastily backed away. "It wasn't me touching you."

"Don't kid yourself." He tossed the apple aside, into the trees, and headed for the motorcycle. She watched as he mounted, pulled the enormous machine upright from the kickstand and took the mirrored sunglasses from his shirt pocket. With a flick of his wrist, he started the engine.

Looking at her, he took a rubber band from around his wrist and tugged his hair into a ponytail, then roared out, wind blowing his shirt against his chest. She watched until the trees swallowed him and the little dirt clearing was silent again.

Moving as if in a dream, Mattie went inside, shut the door and leaned against it. So this was lust, she thought, touching her middle. Good Lord.

She would have let him kiss her. Without an instant of regret or hesitation. When he pulled away, her most acute emotion had been disappointment.

But that was foolish. Very foolish. She didn't have the luxury to indulge some lusty awakening on the part of her body, especially when she had no idea who he was or why he was so interested in her secrets.

A little noise against the window made her whirl, terrified. She stared wildly at the multipaned square, seeking the source of the sound.

She sagged when she saw it was a twig from the pine tree outside the window.

"Mattie," she said aloud, speaking to herself from long habit, "you are an idiot." She began to put away the groceries, slamming them unnecessarily.

Willfully, she called up the night that had sent her running to this invisible little town—called up details she fought to keep tamped down. The memories would give her nightmares, but maybe she needed to be scared a little.

She called up the memory of an after-hours warehouse, the sound of gunfire, and blood. So much blood. She had slipped in it, trying to get away—

Familiar nausea filled her throat with bile. That was enough.

Hiding herself, living a lie, were things Mattie had never attempted. Maybe she was just getting careless and comfortable. If a complete stranger knew she was lying about her name, it was time to get moving. Find some other little town to hide in.

It was Zeke's habit to rise early, one born in childhood when he'd awakened to help his mother weed the garden, knowing it would be the only time he could have her to himself in a day.

So even now, when his work was in the evenings and sometimes ran very late, he found himself wide-awake as dawn broke the night sky. Over the past months, he'd developed a habit of going to the canyon, knowing that if he got there early enough, as with his mother, he'd have it to himself.

Of all the flyspecks on the map he'd blown through the past eighteen months, Kismet would be the hardest for him to leave behind, a thought that bothered him this morning—just a little. He had a rule about getting attached to things. When you got attached, you got in trouble. People, animals, places—he didn't let himself get too comfortable with any of them. Probably time to move on.

But this morning, he was here, and that was good. He stripped at the edge of the river, taking deep pleasure in the brush of cool morning air against his skin. Overhead, a tangle of larks and sparrows sang to the light, as if it were a unique event. He smiled at them, standing on the bank for a moment to brace himself. Taking a deep breath, he touched his stomach in preparation, and with a whoop, jumped into a deep pool.

The water was a biting, icy shock—exhilarating as it stabbed through his hair and needled his flesh. He touched bottom and pushed himself back up, then lazily paddled in the broad pool, admiring the colors around him.

Back in Mississippi, rivers were wide and muddy and slow, as if the heat sucked their energy from them. Their banks were covered with cattails and grass. This river was crystal clear and mountain-cold and ran fast through the canyon it had carved from red sandstone. There was no mud to speak of, because the streambed was the rock itself.

The beauty of it was that the water had played capricious games with the soft rock, creating slides and carving pools and ignoring little flats, with no rhyme

or reason. Later in the day, it would be crowded with
tourists, come from the campgrounds nearby to enjoy the miracle.

He kicked out and submerged himself again, now
used to the invigorating cold. He looked at the sky,
vividly blue above the red of the rocks, and wondered
that such color could exist.

It was only then that he became aware of a prickling uneasiness. With a flush of embarrassment, he
wondered if some campers had wandered over. He'd
been coming here since summer started and had never
been discovered. After a few weeks, he'd shed his cutoffs in favor of skinny-dipping just because it seemed
natural to do so in such a place. Keeping himself covered to the shoulders, he spun around slowly, peering
into the trees at one side of the water. Nothing moved
but a squirrel, who chattered in some irritation at
Zeke's gall invading the quiet so early. He grinned to
himself, relieved, and splashed backward to lean on a
rock in the warming sunlight.

It was only then he caught sight of her, standing at
the foot of a path that probably led straight back to
her little cabin.

Mary. He wiped water from his face and straightened. "Well, well, well," he said. "I'm just runnin'
into you all over the place."

She carried a small paper bag and a thermos. "I
come here every morning to eat my breakfast," she
said, and pointed to a small outcropping of rocks on
the other side of the stream. A natural staircase led to
the perch. "I won't bother you."

"Maybe I'll bother you."

"I doubt it." He saw that it took some effort, but
she resolutely headed toward the perch, leaving her

sandals at the edge of the stream to splash through the shallows to the stairs. When she reached the top, she settled herself primly with her bag in her lap. "You mind your business and I'll mind mine."

Zeke half smiled. She probably had no idea he'd left his clothes in a pile at the edge of the water, or she wouldn't be quite so calm. The pool he stood in was deep enough to cloak his nakedness, but if he moved at all, the clear water wouldn't hide much. "Nice sentiment," he said, "but we've got a little problem."

"What's that?"

"Well, Miss Mary, all my clothes are over there on the bank."

A flash of something crossed her face—satisfaction? She raised her eyebrows. "I guess you'll have to wait until I'm finished with my breakfast to finish your swim, then, won't you?"

Zeke licked his bottom lip. It had been a mistake to underestimate this woman. She might look young and naive, but there was something hard as barbed wire running beneath it all. If he hadn't been so rattled by that mouth yesterday, he would have realized it, too.

"Not necessarily."

She shrugged, cracking open a peanut. Her composure was utterly unrattled this morning, and he wondered what had brought about the change.

"I think you're pretty mad at me, aren't you?"

"Why would I be mad? You deliberately tried to embarrass me at the restaurant, then you followed me home, dropped all these innuendos, then made it sound like I was the one who initiated things." A blaze of color touched her cheeks. "Not to mention the fact you stuck your nose in where it didn't belong."

"All right, all right." He raised a hand. "You're right. I'm sorry."

Sunlight angled through the high trees and over the canyon wall to strike her face. "I'll turn around if you want to get out."

"Much obliged."

She stood up, and Zeke frowned over her clothes—a dowdy pair of baggy shorts with an equally dowdy, baggy tank top. He winced at the waste of that body in those clothes as she turned around, putting her back to him.

For a moment, he paused, struck by the tenderness of her nape. He followed the path of her spine downward to the barely visible outline of her rear end, down farther over the taut thighs and strong calves, tanned to a deep golden hue.

"You'd better hurry up," she warned. "I'm not going to stand here waiting forever."

Zeke pushed out of the water and dashed for the bank, feeling a little tightening of his muscles as he scrambled into his briefs and cutoffs. Much as he hated to do it, he tugged his shirt on, too. Cover the scars.

He turned around and saw to his relief she was still standing with her back to him. "All right," he called.

She settled once more on her perch. "Maybe you shouldn't be out here skinny-dipping."

He waded through the shallows toward her, even though he told himself he ought to be moving in the opposite direction. "You're the first person who has ever come here."

"There's not really room for two up here," she said as he began to climb up the slope.

"Sure there is. Move your fanny over."

She scooted like a little brown mouse, her mirth and bravado shrinking as he sat down next her. He chuckled. "What's wrong, Miss Mary? You scared of the giant?"

"I'm afraid of falling off here."

"You could sit on my lap."

"I think not." To avoid his eyes, she dug in her bag and came up with a handful of peanuts in their shells.

"Some breakfast," he commented and grabbed the bag to peer inside. Peanuts, another apple, a paper carton of orange juice and a small thermos. "Will you share?"

"Help yourself."

He held up the thermos. "Is this coffee?"

She nodded. "But I'm afraid it has cream. I never did learn to like it black."

"That's okay, Miss Mary. I'll drink it your way."

She didn't make a response, just cracked open a peanut and picked out the nuts from within. As he poured a cupful of the still-steaming brew, he caught her sidelong glance sweeping over his bare legs.

"So, what are you doing up so early?" he asked.

"I have to be to work at five-thirty. Even on my days off, I can't sleep past four." A shadow crossed her eyes, and she was suddenly not with him here on the sandstone table, but lost somewhere inside herself. He narrowed his eyes and wondered again what she was hiding. A violent husband? Maybe. It was plain she was scared to death.

He restrained himself from asking any more questions, however. Bad enough he'd crawled up here to sit with her. "I like early morning," he said, admiring the sky. "Private, quiet, peaceful."

"I never knew I did until—" She broke off, bowing her head in consternation.

"I'm not gonna pry this morning," he said quietly. "Promise."

She raised wide brown eyes. "I never got up this early before I started working at the restaurant. I guess you do it all the time?"

"Pretty much." He cracked a peanut and poured the nuts into his palm. "You ever wait tables before?"

A small, rueful smile touched her mouth. "No. It wasn't a pleasant sight the first few days."

He chuckled. "Roxanne train you?"

"Yes. She was so patient, too. She never yelled at me once."

"She's a good lady. Good waitress, too."

Mattie looked at him, and he could see her weighing something in her mind. "She—um—rather likes you." She pinched an earlobe. "That's not really the right word, but you know what I mean."

"Yeah."

"It's not mutual?"

"Are you matchmaking, Miss Mary?"

With a little shrug, she tossed the stem of an apple into the water. "Maybe."

He inclined his head, wondering why she would take that role when he'd been getting pretty clear signals that she "liked" him, as she put it. He touched her bare arm with one finger, liking the silky pale flesh and the jolt it gave her. "Why don't you matchmake me with you?" he drawled. "Might be more successful."

She didn't look at him. "You aren't my type, and I'm not yours."

Only yesterday, Zeke had told himself the same thing. Two different worlds, life-styles, values, everything. But he found his gaze wandering over the smooth length of her long neck, down to the shadow he could glimpse between her breasts, over her smooth, pretty legs.

"How do you know until you try?" he said.

She turned her head, and now she was so close, Zeke could see the green and blue and yellow flecks in the brown irises. "I know," she said, but the huskiness in her voice betrayed her.

Below their dangling feet, the water rushed merrily over the rocks. Birds twittered and cheeped. A soft breeze, smelling of all the best of the outdoors, swept a lock of her hair over her forehead. Zeke let his fingers trace her upper arm and fall into the hollow of her elbow, tracing the path his fingers took with his eyes. An abrupt and insistent heat spread through his groin.

It would be so easy to disarm her, he thought. She was ready to fall right now. All he had to do was lean forward and press his mouth someplace that would surprise her—the sensitive hollow below her ear, the edge of her shoulder, her palm.

She swayed just a little toward him, and the motion brought Zeke to his senses. Alarmed, he snatched his hand away and swore softly.

He'd done it again.

In one day, this soft little mouse of a woman had tempted him into all kinds of thoughts he didn't let himself have. He shook his head. Just hungry, he guessed. A man couldn't go without forever, after all. Obviously, he was getting to the end of his celibacy.

But it would be a mistake to let himself go with this woman. A big mistake.

"I gotta go."

He turned and scrambled down the rock, skinning his heel in his haste to get away from her.

"Zeke?" She climbed down after him, running a little to catch up. "Wait a minute."

He steeled himself and spun around, pasting an annoyed look on his face to discourage anything sweet coming from her.

It worked. A little bit, anyway. She stopped a foot away, her bare feet sunk to the ankles in silvery water. She was still too close. He could smell her shampoo and see a gleam of that innocent hunger in her big brown eyes as she stared up at him. Way, way up, because she wasn't real tall and Zeke didn't meet many men bigger than he was.

"I'm sorry," she said. "I didn't mean to imply you were—" she shrugged. "I don't mean that you're not good enough or anything like that. I'm just not your type."

He took a breath. "You're right. And I'm not yours." He stuck out a hand to shake. "Friends?"

She smiled, and the expression was dazzling, innocent and sweet and damnably delectable. She stuck out her hand. Zeke caught sight of her burns again. It triggered that odd sense of déjà vu and as he took her hand, he turned it over quizzically. "How'd you get these burns, honey?"

She sighed and lifted her hands in front of her. "A teddy bear," she said. "My parents were killed in a house fire when I was six. I was there, too, but the firemen got me out in time, but they couldn't get the bear away from me in time. It stuck to me."

Ah, hell. Now if that wasn't just about the saddest story he'd ever heard—

Irritated with himself, he frowned. "Why do I think I know you? It's driving me crazy."

Her face drained of expression and she backed away. "I don't know. And I'm not going to talk about it again." She whirled and splashed back toward her rock.

Good. That was that. He stalked through the trees without a second glance. Time to get out of town, all right. Trouble was brewing. He could smell it.

Chapter 3

Late that afternoon, Mattie counted her stash. Sixty-seven dollars and forty-eight cents, including dimes and nickles. Not enough.

Restlessly she paced the room, trying to come up with some plan. She had to get out of Kismet, and quickly, or Zeke Shephard was going to have her spilling her secrets like a bag of marbles. And that she simply could not afford.

But sixty-seven dollars wouldn't carry her very far on the bus, and in spite of all the changes in her life the past few weeks, she couldn't see herself hitchhiking.

There was no one to call for help, no one who might loan her money, no one with whom she could seek refuge. All she had was sixty-seven dollars, a passel of ugly clothes and her wits.

She snorted softly to herself. Her wits. Right. Her wits—or lack of them—were what had landed her in this mess in the first place. If she'd used her wits, she would be happily typing letters and organizing the files of the English department at the university, taking night classes toward a degree in English poetry, instead of running for her life and working as a waitress.

"Damn!" she said aloud and slammed a hand down on the table. Her neat stacks of quarters shivered and clinked into disarray.

She cursed the day she had laid eyes on Brian Murphy, cursed the fact she had not seen the truth of him sooner, cursed her own silly weak hunger for a life and family of her own. Looking back, it was incredible that she had actually believed he could offer her anything. It was idiotic that she'd not questioned his wealth sooner, that she hadn't seen how shady some of his friends were. She'd even seen a gun in his glove box and hadn't thought anything of it.

Stupid.

She blew out a long breath and flicked aside the curtain to watch a family of tourists drag their suitcases inside the cabin next door. Three kids in shorts and good tennis shoes, a mother laughing and calling out cautions, a dad grumbling. So normal.

That's what Brian had seemed to be. Normal. She'd met him at Mass, for heaven's sake. Every Sunday, he brought his mother, who had trouble driving. Mattie had noticed him a long time before they spoke. A healthy, tall redhead with a smattering of freckles and merry Irish eyes, he never seemed to mind his duty. Sat calmly with his mother, helped her to the front for Communion, kept her arm tucked in his when they left the church.

Everyone at St. Pius loved Brian Murphy. He'd turned his father's failing trucking business around in a few short years and gave generously to the church from the profits. He had a big family and a sweet way with children, and he'd seemed to think Mattie was the prettiest woman he'd ever laid eyes on.

Well, her hair, anyway. He had practically worshiped her hair.

From the start, Mattie had fallen for his charm and his intention to make an honest woman of her. Like Mattie, Brian wanted many children. He wanted a wife who devoted herself to making a home, though he didn't object to her dabbling, as he put it, in poetry.

Thinking of it now, it sounded so patronizing, but above all things in life, Mattie wanted a family of her own. People to love. Children to tend. Pets shedding hair she could vacuum. She wanted the wildness of the Murphy family holidays.

Even now, the loss of those dreams ached.

Had he ever intended for her to find out the true nature of his business? She didn't think so. The clues had been there all along, if she'd been less eager to dismiss the odd phone calls, the guns he kept everywhere—in his glove box and a drawer in his office and the cupboard at his house, the strange people with whom he sometimes did business.

Once she *had* become suspicious for a little while. It was money that tipped her off—he simply had too much of it. Murphy Trucking was a successful business, but successful enough to support the purchase of a Jaguar? A rambling home in an exclusive neighborhood? Trips to exotic places on a quarterly basis?

He convinced her he'd simply done very canny investing with the help of a good broker. A reasonable explanation.

But a lie, as she now knew.

She found out that Murphy Trucking operated on two levels—the upfront transport of all sorts of goods, from tomatoes to furniture, and the not-so-upfront transport of illegal goods. Mattie still didn't know exactly what. Guns or drugs, most likely.

In the whole mess, Mattie was grateful for one thing: she'd learned in time. It made her sick to imagine herself marrying him, bearing his children and finding out ten years from now her husband was a criminal and murderer.

The night that had changed her life, she'd seen what Brian was capable of—coldblooded murder. She had also seen the rage in his eyes when she fled. If he found her, he would kill her.

It was that simple.

Sixty-seven dollars wasn't enough. Mattie stared at the quarters as if concentration might make them multiply.

Jamie flashed through her mind—Jamie Andersen, her foster brother, the one and only person who'd taken even a passing interest in her at any of the series of foster homes in which she lived from the time of her parents' deaths when she was six until she found her own place when she was sixteen.

Jamie. She chewed the inside of her lip. He'd learned every hustle there was in reform schools and in the streets of Kansas City. Some of them he taught to Mattie in order to keep her safe, so she'd never fall prey to the dark-hearted men of the world.

Wryly, Mattie wondered if Jamie would have seen through Brian. Probably.

To give Mattie something she could always use, anywhere, anytime, Jamie gave her a survival skill of her own. In the smoky dark rooms of riverfront pool halls, Jamie taught Mattie the secrets of the stick. "You never know," he'd told her, a cigarette dangling from his lips, "when your back will be against the wall. Stay in practice and you'll never be sorry."

Her back was against the wall.

"You were right, big brother," she said aloud, wondering if his spirit could hear her. "I'm not sorry." She scooped the money into her bag and slung the weight over her shoulder. There were a few things she had to do, the first being a ride to Flagstaff. Maybe Roxanne would take her.

That night, Southern rock and roll filled the steamy kitchen, blasting from the jukebox at Bronco's. Flipping hamburgers, Zeke sang along with the Allman Brothers. With an artful twist, he tossed a patty into the air, caught it deftly on a big metal spatula and chuckled. Cooking wasn't something he'd choose for his life's work, but it could be kind of a kick at times.

Onions sizzled in the grease, sending their fragrance richly into the air. He slapped cheese on three hamburgers, rescued the buns from their toasting on the other side of the grill and arranged them on a plate.

"Hey, Ed," he called to the owner, who sat in a narrow office not far from the stove, "I'm hungry. You gonna let me go home sometime tonight, or have you just decided to keep me here forever?"

Ed looked at his watch in surprise. "Sorry, man. Didn't realize it was getting so late. Finish up that order and I'll take over."

The cheese was perfectly melted, and Zeke lovingly stacked the burgers onto the waiting buns. French fries from a basket filled the plates, and Zeke slipped the single onto the pass-out bar along with the ticket.

"This one's mine," he said to Ed, lifting the double burger. He took off his apron. "I had a feeling it was time."

He carried the overflowing plate out into the dimly lit bar, taking a place at the counter to eat.

Over the jukebox, he heard the thin fussy cry of a baby. "Give me a beer, Sue," he said to the bartender.

At her glare, he grinned. "Please."

Sue fished a brown bottle from the cooler, and twisted off the top with a quick flick of her wrist. As she settled the beer on a napkin before him, she looked toward the line of tall booths against the far wall. "That poor mother. She's exhausted. Look at her."

Zeke looked over his shoulder. A trio of tourists sat miserably in the booth. Mom and Dad and baby. The couple was young, no more than twenty-five. The mother's face was glazed as she stared at her husband eating the hamburger Zeke had just made. The dad, too, looked frazzled. His hair was uncombed and a smear of black grease stained his forearm. He ate as though he was starving.

The baby, about six months old, just fussed in its mother's arms.

Zeke grabbed a french fry from his plate. "What's their story?"

"Broke down just outside of town. The car's in the shop—Jerry's working on it, but the motel is full. I don't think they were thrilled to have to come into a bar, but there isn't anyplace else open." She smiled wryly. "Poor baby."

Zeke ate slowly, tapping his foot against the floor in time to the music. When he was halfway through the burger, the baby started to scream in earnest, pushing away the bottle his mother tried to give him.

"He sure is tired," Sue said slowly.

With narrowed eyes, he glared at her. "Don't even start, woman."

"But you're so good with babies, and that mother is so tired she can't see straight. Come on—you know you want to."

The baby shrieked and settled into the steady, low crying of pure, miserable exhaustion. Zeke sighed and tossed his napkin down. He stood, ignoring Sue's smile.

With reluctance, he let his feet carry him across the room. "That's one tired youngun," he said to the exhausted couple.

"I'm sorry," the mother said. "Is he bothering you? I just can't calm him down—I think he knows I'm worn-out, too."

She was near tears.

He cleared his throat. "I got five sisters back in Mississippi—why don't you let me take him for you for a minute so you can eat and wash your face?"

Doubt crossed her weary features, and warred with the hope of relief.

"I work here—ask the bartender. I won't go anywhere with him," he said. "I'll just stand right over there and we'll dance a little. Y'all can keep an eye on us." He held out his arms.

The mother looked at the father. He gave her a quick nod. "It can't hurt, honey. Go wash your face and order a hamburger." He touched her hand. "Have a beer, too."

"If you're sure," she said, looking at Zeke.

He grinned and winked. "Give him here."

The baby had quieted a little at the sound of Zeke's voice. When he took the hefty, soft weight from his mother's arms, the baby was surprised into silence for an instant. He stared up at the stranger holding him with wide blue eyes, swollen and red from crying. "Hey, sweet pea," Zeke said quietly. "Let's go dance a little while. I'll make you feel better."

He wandered a little closer to the jukebox. Another soft bluesy Allman Brothers piece was playing and Zeke started to dance gently, cradling the baby close to his chest. He sang along, quietly, and the baby stared at him in amazement. Zeke grinned. "You're so tired, sweet pea. Come on and go to sleep. Your mama's tired, too."

The baby found his fingers and started to suck. A shuddering breath passed through the round little body as he settled into the crook of Zeke's arm. "Yeah, that's it," he crooned. "Go on to sleep now. I'll just dance awhile with you."

He started to sing again, quietly. From the corner of his eye, he saw the mother slip into the ladies' room. Her husband called the waitress over. From behind the bar, Sue grinned at Zeke, shaking her head.

He looked back at the small face. Through half-open eyes, the baby looked back. For just a minute, Zeke felt lost in time. How many times had he rocked his sisters this way, helping his mother? Or held a cousin while an uncle danced with some girl?

Give the baby to Zeke. He'll take care of it.

And he always did. He had a weakness for babies. All of them—their sweet round faces and tiny hands and feet, the smell of baby powder and the incredible softness of their cheeks. Only thing as soft as a baby's skin was a woman's breast. He liked the way they went together sometimes, too.

The baby drifted off, but Zeke kept dancing and singing quietly. No hurry. The mother emerged from the bathroom, a little calmer, and she smiled in gratitude. He nodded.

With a sigh, he looked back into the baby's face. "I got you, sweet pea," he murmured, and touched the downy head.

His only regret in life was the lack of babies to cuddle. But he'd vowed a long time ago there would be none. Ever. Babies had to grow up and suffer and he just couldn't stand it. He'd fled Mississippi after watching too many suffer at the hands of those who supposedly loved them the most.

But that didn't mean he couldn't enjoy holding one now and again. With a smile, he swayed lazily along with the music, comforted someplace deep inside by the round softness against his chest.

"Oh, good grief," Roxanne said as she pushed in the door of the bar.

"What?" Mattie asked, coming in behind her.

"Look at that."

"What?" Mattie scanned the room. It was crowded. That was good. Not all locals; equally good. There were a few people dancing, and a couple of pool games going on in one corner. Mattie smiled. Excellent. But she didn't really know what disgusted Roxanne so much. "What?" she repeated.

Roxanne stepped aside and lifted her chin in the direction of the jukebox. Two couples danced close together on the little cleared section of floor, a common enough sight.

And then Mattie saw him. Zeke. Swaying gently in time with the music, a baby cradled in the crook of his arm. He wore a sleeveless black T-shirt that left his powerful, muscular arms bare, and the tiny head of the baby looked as if it could be crushed if Zeke bent his elbow.

Except there was such gentleness in his hold, and his head bent over the sleeping child to murmur sweet nothings. Mattie watched his mouth move.

Yesterday in the restaurant, she'd seen his sex appeal and roughness. At her house, she'd seen his danger. This morning, at the river, she'd seen his beauty and teasing, and again that danger.

Of all of them, the tenderness she saw now was the most compelling. And terrifying.

With some alarm, she looked at Roxanne. "I don't think I want to stay here, after all."

"Oh, don't be silly. Where are we going to go? The Plaza?" She grabbed Mattie's arm and pulled her into the room. "I'm sick of being cooped up in my house."

Mattie kept her eyes averted as they settled in a booth and ordered a beer. She wasn't much of a drinker, but beer and Kismet seemed to go together, and there were rules about the game Jamie had taught her. A beer in hand was important.

From the corner of her eye, she watched Zeke take the baby back to its mother, then take a seat at the bar. "You think he did that for effect?" Roxanne asked.

"What?"

"Danced with a baby."

Mattie frowned. "Why would he do it on purpose?"

"Well, it's a known fact that women can't resist a man who likes children. Maybe he's got his eye on the bartender."

Mattie shrugged. She'd already spent too much time thinking about Zeke Shephard, as it was; she didn't want to get drawn in now. Deliberately, she shifted to get a better view of the pool tables.

A tourist with a sunburned nose played cheerfully, sipping a beer and nodding his head in time with the music. A recreational player, and probably a father with kids to get back home, too. No good.

His opponent was thirtyish, a local who worked on the road crew. He smiled at her. Mattie waved. He was single, with plenty of money to spend, and he probably dropped at least a third of his paycheck in this bar every week. He also played well, with honed concentration and a sharp break.

Roxanne tapped her arm. "I didn't come here with you to talk to myself, you know," she said curtly.

"I'm sorry," Mattie said pleasantly, as if life and death did not hang in the balance. "I just like pool. Do you play?"

"A little. Not too well." She sipped her beer with a dark glance toward the bar. "How do you think he got that tattoo?"

"Are we back to Zeke again?"

Roxanne grinned, and the strained look of peevishness disappeared. "Yes. Do you think I can't see how carefully you're ignoring him?" She shook her head. "I can't believe what a dress and a haircut did for you."

Mattie touched her hair, pleased with the sleek swinging feel of her new cut. "You like it?"

"It looks great." She eyed Mattie's new dress, too. "And I love the dress. With a body like that, I'd wear skintight everyday."

Mattie shrugged. She never wore skintight clothes, and even this new dress was a bit too risqué for her usual taste, but there wasn't much selection in her price range or in the tiny little shop she'd found. It would do the job; that was all she cared about. If Roxanne thought she'd dressed up for Zeke, all the better.

"So," Roxanne prodded, "how do you think he got that tattoo?"

Mattie wanted to get back to her examination of the games in progress, and Zeke was in her line of vision. She examined the tattoo impassively, an exquisitely rendered stallion that emblazoned his right shoulder. "Same way everyone else gets one," she said. "With a needle."

"You know what I mean. What possesses a person to sit down and let somebody stick a needle in their arm like that, over and over?"

Mattie had seen what she needed to see of the remaining pool players, and she looked back to Zeke's tattoo. The sight of it, moving with the muscles in his arms, sent a sharp tiny spiral of heat through her middle, and she hastily tore her gaze away. "I don't know," she said, turning back to Roxanne. "Why don't you ask him?" She slid out of the booth. "I'm going to play pool."

This was the hard part for Mattie, the walk through the room in her close-fitting dress. She'd learned how important it was, but it shamed her to know the men in the room were examining her body—looking at her breasts and hips and legs as if she were fried chicken.

Jamie had insisted she learn how to do it; he had forced her to try making the game work in a loose pair of jeans and old blouse and no makeup.

It didn't work nearly as well.

There was only one really bad moment this time. Zeke caught sight of her as she neared his spot at the bar. His face didn't change, but she saw a hard, cynical shimmer light his eyes.

"Well, Miss Mary," he said in greeting. "Looks like I underestimated you all the way around." His gaze swept her head to toe and back again. "Guess you do know the rules."

His mouth was tight, as if he was disappointed, and it was nearly enough to send her scuttling right back to her spot at the table with Roxanne.

Instead, she met the judgment in those harsh pale eyes and called up a memory of three men lying in their own blood in a warehouse in Kansas City. She squared her shoulders. "You bet," she said, and passed him. Her thigh brushed his knee.

At the pool table, she grinned at the man she knew from the café. "I've been watching. You play pretty well."

"Thanks. You play?"

This was the critical moment. Jamie always wanted her to pretend she couldn't play until the stakes were high. She never could fake bad pool well enough, nor did she feel comfortable with a true hustle. "Yes," she said honestly. "Five dollars a game?"

His eyebrows rose in surprise. "You sure, honey? I've been playin' since I was three years old. Not many folks can beat me."

Mattie smiled. "I can."

The game was on.

Chapter 4

From his perch on the bar stool, Zeke watched Mary in action, cursing himself for believing she was an innocent anything. How could he have been so blind?

Tonight she looked as sweet as an ice cream sundae in her blue dress and bare legs. And she knew it, knew it in the way she moved her body as she studied the table; knew just exactly where men were looking when she bent over, just exactly how little attention they were paying her game and just exactly how far to push before pulling back.

Why the hell was he so disappointed?

The dress, to her credit, wasn't particularly suggestive. Women all around him wore a lot worse. It was a simple blue T-shirt knit, belted at the waist, with a modest scoop neckline. Short sleeves and plenty of room to move in.

It was the way she wore the damn thing that was so alluring. Her hips swayed, and her breasts moved gently, and when she bent over to take a shot, he could glimpse just the smallest expanse of creamy flesh. Just enough to tantalize, not enough to satisfy.

She was a pro. He drank beer, watching her manipulate the macho boys clustering around to watch and place bets and wait for their turn to play. They didn't care if they lost, and Mary knew it.

Once, she caught sight of him staring at her, and she blushed. At least she had the grace to look ashamed, he thought darkly.

He didn't know why he sat there so long. His shift was over. He could have gone home any time. But he couldn't seem to make himself take that first step. Like every other idiot male in the joint, he was transfixed.

She didn't act like a siren or a coy courtesan—she wasn't even the slightest bit beautiful except for those pretty lips and big eyes—just played a good game of pool over and over again, winning consistently. No one could beat her, and the more she won, the more they wanted to try. The stakes went up as some of the challengers drank a little more. She met them all with friendly smiles and good grace.

By one, Zeke had enough. He stood up and counted out a hundred dollars. "I'm next," he said. "You've all had a chance to beat the lady. Let me show you how to do it."

Mary met his eyes. No fear. But he caught the flicker of her eyes on the stack of bills in his hand. She lifted a shoulder. "You can try."

He stuck his cigarette in the corner of his mouth and chose a stick from the wall, holding it up to eye level to check the true. She watched him calmly, but he could see she was a little more tense by the time he rounded the table.

The bartender blinked the lights. Last call. Zeke waved at her to bring two beers.

The crowd had already thinned, and at this signal, most of the rest of the watching group shook their heads and ambled away. "Let us know, Zeke," called one, "if you beat her. I want to see how it's done tomorrow."

Mary stood by the table, her cue clutched before her. When Sue delivered the beers, he made a show of giving Mary hers. "Thought that other one might be getting a little warm by now."

She slid a guilty look toward the half-full bottle. "Maybe a little." Glancing around, she said, "It's getting awfully late. We can meet tomorrow to play this game if you want to."

Zeke shook his head slowly. Unless he sorely missed his guess, Miss Mary would be halfway to Timbuktu by tomorrow evening. "Nope. I lock up most nights, anyway."

She lifted an eyebrow in concession. "Your break."

"Let's play a warm-up, first, shall we?" It was a measured ploy—maybe she'd take it, maybe she wouldn't. He watched her weigh the choice, biting on the inside of her cheek as she looked at him through narrowed eyes.

He could almost see the gears turning. If she played him cold, she might lose because she didn't know his game. She wasn't fool enough not to take him seriously. On the other hand, a warm-up game might give him an edge.

"All right," she said, evidently opting to check out his game. "One warm-up."

He'd watched her through innumerable games over the evening and had learned a lot more than she would have liked. Her bank shots were a little weak. Not much, but enough. She didn't get cocky or lose her edge when she was winning, and that was to her benefit because she could shift a hip just so and an opponent might be more interested in the play of her legs than the table.

She was very, very good. Honorable if you didn't count the sweet curves beneath her modest and all-too-alluring dress. And that honor would be her downfall.

Zeke didn't have but one rule about pool: he played to win. Even after drinking a little bit more than his share, his wits were sharp, and he was irritated enough by her manipulations tonight that he thought she deserved to be taught a lesson.

The first game, he held back. Missed a shot or two, carefully. A bank shot that missed by a sixteenth of an inch; a corner shot that bounced on the edge.

She won with the eight ball, but it could have gone either way. As she bent over the black number eight, he found his attention straying to the simple straight muscle in her upper arm, noticing the sleek way it moved as she shot. Her hair swung forward, the brown strands taking on a golden shimmer as the light over the table struck it.

He mentally shook himself. Damn. He knew what she was doing and fell for it, anyway.

"I'm leaving," Sue called. "I already checked the back door."

"Thanks, honey. See you tomorrow." Zeke looked around in satisfaction. The bar was empty. He crossed the room and locked the door behind Sue, then took a couple of dollars in quarters out of his pocket and dropped them in the jukebox.

Then he turned and met Mary's gaze with a small grin. "You nervous?" he asked.

She straightened. "No."

"Good. Let's play."

It was the hardest game of pool she'd ever played in her life. Mattie had been lulled a little by his warm-up game, and it had been a mistake. Now she didn't dare let down her guard. If he took her for a hundred dollars, she'd be in sorry shape, and had already tipped her hand in this little town. She'd have to go to Flagstaff and start over. The idea made her feel ill.

Now he bent over the table, eyeing a tough bank shot for the two-ball. Light from the fixture hanging low over the table swam over his flesh in long, loving strokes, catching on the sheen of sweat that glossed his skin and caressed his muscles, each and every one.

He was the best player in the bar tonight, and like Jamie, he was dangerous. He didn't care about hurting someone who was game enough to play. He played ruthlessly and played to win.

He swung back to shoot and she closed her eyes tight to whisper a prayer. "Oh, please, let him miss!"

The clunk of a ball falling home told her he hadn't. With a sigh, she opened her eyes to check the damages. The eight ball hung on the edge of the corner pocket. A whisper would knock it in.

Zeke picked up the chalk and lazily rolled it over the tip of his cue. He gave her a slow grin. "Well, Miss Mary, it looks bad for your side."

She glanced at the table and shrugged. "Win some, lose some."

"We could go double or nothing." He bent over, and with a graceful move, nudged the cue ball to kiss the eight. It tumbled home.

"I don't have that much money," she said. It wasn't strictly true, but she sure didn't have enough to gamble two hundred dollars.

"Sure you do." He rounded the table to stand in front of her. "I saw you tucking it away in your shoe all night."

The jukebox, which had been playing steadily, suddenly clicked off, plunging the room into thick silence. And suddenly, Mattie was aware that she was alone with this man in the middle of the night in a locked bar. Desperate straits, even for her.

Don't ever let 'em know they've got you.

It was as if Jamie were right there speaking to her, and his words steadied her nerves. As calmly as she was able, she met Zeke's pale gaze. "I said I don't choose to play again."

"Is that right." He stepped a little closer, huge as a giant, his broad, burly shoulders blocking her view.

She forced herself to stand her ground. "That's right."

He smiled. It was a dangerous, deeply sexual smile. "A hundred dollars is a pretty big sum of money to lose," he said. With one finger, he reached out to stroke her arm, and his gaze followed the movement over her skin. She felt every millimeter of the journey, but forced herself not to react.

"It's a risk you take." She shifted to put her cue aside. "I have to go."

His hand curled around her arm. "Not yet."

Violently, Mattie jerked away. "You've got your money. What do you want?"

"I'll make you a deal."

She crossed her arms. "What deal?"

Again he stepped closer, and Mattie felt an irrational sense of disappointment. He was going to offer to cancel the debt in trade for sex. In spite of some of her fear of him, she'd thought him a cut above that.

And yet, her eyes caught on his lips and she couldn't help wishing she could kiss him just once, to see what it was like. He had the most beautiful mouth she'd ever seen on a man. Firm and sensual, as if there was no end to the pleasures it could give. As she watched, the corners of that mouth quirked into a little smile.

"No, Miss Mary," he said. "Not that. I already told you I have rules about good girls."

"You are the most arrogant man I've ever met," she said in a wondering tone. "Why do you think every woman you run into wants to go to bed with you?"

"I don't." He grinned and edged one step closer, so close she could feel his extraordinary heat. "But you're a liar if you tell me you haven't given the notion some thought."

She looked at him, about to tell him just that. But she was caught in the pale sea-color of his eyes, and for the first time she noticed how thick and dark his lashes were.

His face changed as she stared at him. His lids grew sleepy and his mouth softened, and he edged closer still. His enormous hand curled around the back of her neck.

"You've got the most kissable lips I've ever seen in my life," he said quietly.

Her breath caught and her body stilled in an agony of waiting. She became aware of his earthy scent, and then everything was blotted out by his mouth.

His mouth. It touched hers lightly, just touched at first. And it seemed every nerve in her body suddenly rushed toward her mouth to join the explosion of sensation his lips brought. He moved his head and his mouth slid one way, then the other, and his fingers tightened around her neck, pulling her closer.

He suckled her lower lip with a lazy kind of savoring, then moved with the same slow hunger to her upper. She found her hands on his arms and wasn't sure if she was bracing herself or had just lost her mind entirely, but she couldn't pull away.

She couldn't resist tasting him, exploring him. Hungrily she moved, testing the curve and shape and pliant give of his mouth; she let her tongue inch out to tease the edge, just to see how it felt against hers.

Zeke made a low sound in his throat, and she found herself abruptly free, staring again into his harsh and compelling face. For a long moment, he simply looked at her intently, then pulled away, shaking his head.

"Damn," he said, shoving his hand through his hair. "That wasn't what—I didn't..."

He whirled and grabbed the money from their bet off the bar. With a violent gesture, he flung it all on the pool table. "I know you've got trouble and you need this money. Just tell me who you are, and I'll let you walk away with every single penny."

Mattie stared at him, at the money settling in scattered little flutters on the table and the floor. One twenty-dollar bill landed on her toe.

In an agonized whisper, she asked, "Why do you care? Why can't you just leave me alone?"

"I don't know." He sighed. "It bugs me that I can't remember why I know you. It seems—" he frowned "—important."

Mattie didn't wait to hear any more. She whirled and ran for the door. She grabbed the handle and yanked. Futilely. A dead bolt held it firm. With a soft sound of panic, she tugged again.

"I've got the key." Zeke came up behind her. "If you'll get the hell out of the way, I'll open it for you."

She schooled herself to step back, watching as he turned the key and jerked open the door with a sharp, annoyed gesture. "Go on, now," he said. "Run on home, Miss Mary."

Something in that derisive tone chased away her fear. "I forgot something," she said, and squatted to take the money out of her shoe. With a gesture as patronizing as she could manage, she tucked the bills into his shirt pocket.

Or tried. He dodged out of reach when he realized her intent. "C'mon, Mary. Keep it."

"You won it fair and square." Firmly, she stuffed it in the pocket and brushed by him.

"Mary!"

She ignored him. The thin, dry desert air had a bite this time of night, even in full summer. She should have brought a jacket with her.

"Mary, will you hold on one cotton pickin' minute?"

She kept walking, striking out into the inky blackness of the mountain night without a second thought. At home in Kansas City, she wouldn't have crossed the street by herself this time of night. Here, there was no danger in the three blocks to her little cabin. It was deeply silent and smelled of pines. She would miss that fresh smell and the quiet.

A pithy word bit the night. Mattie heard the door slam. She didn't look back to see if he'd gone inside—surely he wouldn't walk off and leave a hundred dollars scattered over the pool table.

He would. The sound of his bike engine growled into the quiet. Mattie tensed, hearing him approach. He idled up beside her. "I suppose giving you a ride home is out of the question?"

The headlamp on the bike shot a path through the darkness. Mattie followed it, unwilling to admit she wanted the light, liked the comfort of engine noises in the quiet. She spared him a single glance, seeing only the sheen of his skin and the long tumble of his hair.

She kept walking.

"I'll just tag along for my own peace of mind, then."

Mattie stopped. "Zeke, what do you want from me? I wasn't even going to play you a game of pool until you insisted. I gave you the money you won. I haven't done anything to you—why won't you leave me alone?"

The bike stopped when she did and he held upright easily, the engine idling lazily between his legs. "I don't honestly know, Mary. You just seem like you—" He shook his head. "Like you're all alone."

"You're all alone."

"That's different."

"Right. You're a big bad man and I'm just a helpless little woman."

"Partly." He took a cigarette from his shirt pocket as he spoke. "I'm also a lot meaner and tougher than you. You aren't the kind of woman that ought to be hanging out in pool halls and walking home in the dark at all times of night."

"Thank you for your insight." Mattie started walking again.

His voice followed her. "I'll make you a deal, Miss Mary."

"Another one?"

"Just tell me your real first name." He cocked his head, and his smile was coaxing, friendly, sexy. "Just for my own satisfaction."

"And if I do, you'll leave me alone?"

He lit his cigarette. "If you want me to."

There was that arrogance again, in the sure tilt of his head, the half smile on that sensual mouth. The expression said no woman ever refused him anything. She crossed her arms. "Mattie."

He raised his chin, considering. "Matilda?"

"That wasn't part of the deal."

"Fair enough." He grinned. "Hop on. I'll give you a ride."

"Not in this getup."

"Oh, who's gonna see? I won't peek." Restlessly, he flicked his wrist on the accelerator and the bike growled.

The dress was an excuse. No way, after that kiss in the bar, that she wanted to climb up behind him and lean into that long, muscled back. "No."

He shrugged and continued to walk the bike alongside her. For one whole block, neither of them said anything. Mattie would never have admitted it to him, but she liked the low purring of the bike and the lighted path its headlight made. "I can't get over how dark it is here," she said at last.

"Yeah. Makes me think of where I grew up."

Not home. Where he grew up. "Where is that?"

"Little town near Clinton, Mississippi. How 'bout you?"

Without even thinking, Mattie said, "Kansas City. Missouri side."

As soon as the words were out, a stab of cold terror struck her heart. How could she be so careless?

All at once, the evening overwhelmed her. Zeke had unnerved her with his pool game, his kiss, his big motorcycle and lazy drawl. Close to tears, she said, "Will you please just leave me alone?"

"Mary—Mattie—I'm sorry." He touched her arm, but she jerked away. "You see what I mean, honey? If I can trip you, someone else can, too."

"Don't you think I know that? Do you think this is normal for me?" She struggled to hold on to her disintegrating emotions, but felt the losing battle in the trembling of her arms. "All I'm trying to do is stay low, stay out of sight and keep moving. And I'd have been able to if you hadn't kept sticking your big nose in where it didn't belong."

They had reached the driveway of the motel. "I don't mean you any harm, Mattie," he said, his voice deep and quiet against the vastness of the night.

Mattie clenched her jaw. "I know." There was a quaver in her voice she loathed—and just the sound of it almost unleashed her tears. Urgently, she stared at the green neon tubing on the office door: Shady Pine Motel. The letters blurred, then cleared as she gained control.

Zeke hadn't moved. If only she could turn to him the way she longed to, finally tell someone all the terrible things she'd seen, release her horror somehow. If only she could tell someone, she wouldn't feel so lonely.

He took her hand. "Take care, Mattie. I won't bother you again."

Something touched her hand, but before she had a chance to see what it was, he'd roared off, taillight blinking red in the darkness.

Mattie opened her palm and saw the neatly folded twenties she'd given him.

Chapter 5

Zeke didn't sleep well or long. By seven, he was up and dressed and headed over to the café, breaking not only several of his own rules—namely to leave good girls alone and to mind his own business—but also his promise to Mattie.

But his instincts were screaming. Rules didn't hold much weight against that.

The café was busy with the breakfast rush, but already the road crews and park police had begun to clear out. Zeke took his customary place at the counter, setting a long white envelope with Mattie's name on it beside the napkin.

"Morning, gorgeous," Roxanne said, automatically filling a heavy ceramic mug with coffee. "How you doing today?"

"All right. Is Mary here?"

"It's her day off. You're stuck with me."

He scowled. Mattie was probably long gone by now. "Damn," he said aloud.

Roxanne lifted an eyebrow. "Come on, now. I'm not that bad a waitress, am I?"

"That's not what I meant." He touched the envelope on the counter. "I've got something for her. She forgot it last night."

"She kicked your butt, too, huh?"

Zeke couldn't tell if she was pleased or annoyed. "I guess."

"I've never seen a woman play pool like that."

"She's good, no question." He sipped his hot coffee. "Where did you go, anyway?"

Roxanne shrugged, and this time, it was plain she was miffed. "As long as she was playing, there was no point to my hanging around."

He chuckled. "Turnabout is fair play. I've seen you hog the attention of every man in the room on more than one occasion."

"Yeah, but she doesn't do it on purpose." She shook her head, giving him a rueful grin. "Meow."

A man called for more coffee. Roxanne lifted a finger to tell him to wait a minute. "You want something to eat?"

Zeke shook his head. "Just the coffee right now."

"All right." With a quirky smile, she added, "If you need anything, just whistle."

There was coffee in his cup, so he might as well drink it. He knew he wouldn't find Mattie and it depressed the hell out of him. She couldn't have had more than two hundred dollars in that shoe of hers, and how could she get by with that? He'd gone back to the bar and collected the money he'd tossed at her, planning to slip it under her door. At the last minute, he'd decided to wait until he could give it to her face-to-face.

Wished he hadn't waited now.

Damn. He'd worried about her all night long, tossing and turning as he tried to figure out how he knew her, and what she was afraid of.

The pieces just didn't hang together. Even given the fact that somebody, somewhere had taught her to hustle pool, Zeke would bet she really was exactly what she seemed, a nice woman from the Midwest who'd done exactly what she was supposed to do all her life. And yet, now she was in enough trouble she had to change her name and hide out in a little town a long way from home.

What kind of trouble could a woman like Mattie possibly find?

There was an easy answer to that question. The only obvious answer: an abusive husband. He thought of her burned hands and the sad story she'd told about them, but he'd told a lie or two about his own scars. No one wanted to admit to having been abused. There was always sick, secret guilt attached.

Restlessly, he stirred his coffee and tapped the spoon on the edge of the cup.

Maybe it wasn't a husband. Maybe it was something else and he just filled in the abusive angle from his own experience.

Whatever it was, it was bad. And whatever Mattie thought, she didn't have the tools to stay hidden long. It wasn't as hard as most people thought to find somebody you really wanted to find. Most folks, and he'd bet a dollar to a doughnut that Mattie was one of them, left clues in a bright red trail behind them.

Damn.

The old need filled him, near to choking. It had grown in childhood, when he was the only one his sisters had. Grimly, he tapped the spoon, watching fat brown drops of coffee fall to the pool below, fighting memories of a cruel and brutal man.

His instincts told him she was in deep trouble. But what had his instincts ever got him? The last time he'd stepped into someone's life like this, it had ended up costing him nearly everything.

Leave it alone.

That would be the smart thing. Unfortunately, smart never seemed to enter into many of his decisions. Impulsively, he asked Roxanne, "What time does the bus come in?"

"About ten or eleven, I think."

He nodded. Probably wasn't any other way out of town for Mattie. Maybe he could still catch her.

And maybe he ought to listen to sense just once in his life. Mattie herself had made it plain she wanted him to mind his own business.

He didn't like trouble. There ought to be a limit, after all, to how much trouble one man had to manage in one lifetime.

As he argued with himself, two men came in and sat at the counter. One was tall, redheaded, with the freckled, wholesome good looks of a popsicle man. The other, though just as well groomed, carried a faintly greasy aura. His hooded eyes scanned the room. Both men wore city ideas of camping gear: chinos and flannel shirts with creases in the sleeve sharp enough to cut bread. Zeke looked at their boots. Clean soles.

They made small talk with the waitress, Cora, an older woman who filled in only on the main wait-

ress's day off. Redhead ordered a cup of coffee and
raved about the beauty of the area in a hearty tone.
Zeke couldn't say why the man's praise rang false, but
his nerves prickled.

Warily, he shifted on the swivel stool and glanced
through the plate-glass window at the front of the
diner, looking for the car the pair had driven. A fancy
El Camino, not a rental.

It had Kansas plates.

Affecting carelessness, Zeke turned back and waved
for a refill on his coffee. Redhead kept talking. "You
know," he told Cora, "we're not really on a pleasure
trip. We've been looking for someone...my sister.
Maybe you've seen her."

Zeke lifted his cup, keeping his eyes on the pass-out
bar as if what they said made no difference to him.

"You got a picture?" Cora asked.

"Sure do. Right here." He pulled out his wallet.

Zeke glanced over, feigning idle curiosity. Redhead
wore a guileless expression, a smile so innocent it
practically shone. The picture he tugged from a cel-
lophane sleeve was too small for Zeke to see from
three stools over.

"She's pretty, isn't she?" Redhead said. "My sister, Mattie O'Neal. She left her boyfriend standing at
the altar and we just want to find her and let her know
everything is okay."

Cora patted her apron pocket for glasses. "Poor
thing," she said.

"You can't tell it in the picture," Redhead said,
"but she has the most gorgeous hair you've ever seen.
Way past her hips, kind of wavy."

With a sudden flash, Zeke remembered why Mattie
looked so familiar—and understood why he couldn't

place her. He also realized Redhead was lying. Moving as lazily as possible, he stood up, dropped a dollar on the counter, picked up the envelope full of money and waved to Roxanne.

As he headed for the door, he heard Redhead say, "Her hands are scarred, too. Burned them with paraffin making candles when she was sixteen."

Zeke walked faster. Just as he reached the front door, Roxanne said, "Burned hands? Mary's hands are burned like that."

The hairs on the back of his neck stiff as teeth, Zeke shoved open the door. Coming in were two guys from the road crew. Both had been in the bar last night.

They trapped him with the open door in his hand. "Zeke Shephard, you dog! Did you manage to beat Mary's game last night?"

Zeke glanced over his shoulder just as Redhead and his sinister pal came to their feet. They stared at him. Redhead's expression was considerably less guileless now.

Zeke pushed through the two men and hopped on his bike, hauling it upright as he turned the key. The engine lit just as the two men came out of the restaurant. By the time Zeke cleared the parking lot, they were in the El Camino.

Mattie rolled her change and stuck it in a sock at the bottom of her huge leather purse, the only thing she had left from her old life. In bills, she counted nine twenties, six fives and twenty-three ones—the spoils of her pool games last night. $233. Not a fortune, but enough to get her out of Kismet.

In a small tote bag were her meager clothes and a bag of toiletries. She added oranges, cheese crackers in little packets, two Butterfingers and a family size pack of gum. Last was a battered paperback copy of Collected English Poets that she had found in the thrift store when she'd bought her shorts. She touched it lovingly as she settled it in the tote.

A small part of her mourned her personal library back home, the well-tended, lovingly preserved books she'd been collecting since high school. A friend had built special shelves for her in the living room of the small apartment. Mattie wondered what would happen to that library now. It wasn't, with its sonnets and poetry and literary criticism, the sort of collection many people would care about.

With a small sigh, she brushed the thought away. The lost library fell into the realm of things she could do nothing about. No point in moaning and groaning about it.

After double-checking to make sure she'd forgotten nothing, she stood by the window of the cheery cabin, visually embracing the view of ferns and pines and majestic red rocks one more time. Before she'd come here, she'd had no idea the world could be so still and quiet a thing; had never dreamed nature offered such a bounty of sensual pleasures. She'd spent her entire life within the confines of Kansas City.

Damn Zeke Shephard, anyway. If it weren't for him, she might have made some kind of life for herself here, far away from anyone she'd ever known. If not for him—

No, it wasn't his fault. She had to be honest enough to admit she had wanted to spill her secrets to him, take him into her confidence.

A pang shot through her chest. In leaving Kismet, she'd be leaving Zeke, too. A part of her knew she would always wonder what it might have been like to let herself go, just once, and experience the promise of dangerous pleasure he exuded like musk.

A wisp of poetry floated through her mind: *How arrives it joy lies slain, and why unblooms the best hope ever sown?*

The extreme melancholy of the quote surprised her. She hadn't realized she felt so strongly about leaving, and even now, she didn't know if it was Zeke or Kismet she would miss. Both.

She wasn't meant to be on the run, transient and alone. All she had ever wanted—ever—was a quiet, safe, simple life with people she loved around her. A family of her own.

Suddenly, into the still golden morning came a sound, a deep growling purr. Coming fast. Mattie moved to the screen door, half annoyed, half distraught. She didn't want to say goodbye to him in person. He'd see straight through her coolness to the silly crush she had on him.

Intolerable thought.

Deciding to take the offense, Mattie opened the door and stepped onto the porch just as Zeke pulled up. His hair, unrestrained by the usual ponytail he wore when riding, was wild and tangled. He kicked off the bike, glanced over his shoulder and leaped up to the porch.

"Zeke—"

"There's a redheaded man down at the café looking for a woman with very long hair and scarred hands. Anybody you know?"

An abrupt and overwhelming fear stole the breath from Mattie's lungs. She stared at Zeke in horror. "At the café?"

"And coming this way fast." He grabbed her arms, spun her around. "Grab your purse and let's get you out of here."

Mattie didn't question the order. She grabbed the tote and her purse from the bed and dashed out, leaving the door open in her haste to be away. Zeke had already started the bike. Mattie got on behind him and he handed her a helmet. "We'll sort everything out later. Just put this on and hang on tight."

"Go," she urged, tugging on the helmet.

He was already moving.

Mattie had never been on a motorcycle in her life. Instinctively, she pressed close to Zeke and followed the light lean of his body as they banked into a turn. His hair whipped her face.

The motel parking lot was gravel, on a downslope. Speed was impossible. As he turned into the driveway that led to the highway, Mattie heard him swear.

"What?"

"Hold on tight and keep your head down. This is about to get ugly."

Over his shoulder, Mattie caught a glimpse of a sky blue El Camino before the bike surged forward. Her heart thundered as they roared past the vehicle. Brian, plain as day, sat behind the wheel, his face murderous as they passed him.

Then the bike was rocketing down the highway. To keep from flying off, Mattie grabbed hard to Zeke's waist. Waves of cold sweat flashed over her at the feeling of speed whipping against them. The trees and hillsides were a blur of color. The wind made a high noise. Tiny stings struck her bare arms—maybe rocks or little bugs.

And she held on with all her might.

A strange volley of noise pricked her attention. A ping and a deeper thud—

"Keep your head down," Zeke yelled.

At the side of the road a chunk of pavement went flying.

Bullets.

"Oh, God!" She buried her face against Zeke's back, closing her eyes. A shudder rushed down her exposed spine and she thought of Zeke's bare head.

The bike seemed to suddenly leap from the road, and for one terrified moment, Mattie had no idea what was happening. She thought wildly that Zeke had been shot and they were flying off the road, out of control.

Then she realized he'd veered off the highway to a slim path in the woods. The jolt of the rough road yanked her head up—and she was promptly slapped by a pine branch. The stinging blow caught her across the nose and right cheek and brought tears to her eyes.

"Keep your head down!"

Mattie ducked into his back.

The bike jumped and skidded and gave off deep, annoyed growlings. Against her arms and chest, Mattie felt Zeke's powerful body fighting to control the machine. He flung out a leg on one side, then the other; she felt him duck and heard the scrape of a thick branch on her helmet. The muscles of his torso flexed and contracted. Between her legs, she felt the tension of his hips.

Slowly, she grew aware that there were no noises behind them, that the only sound *anywhere* was the bike as it leaped and jumped. Cautiously, she looked behind them.

They were on a narrow path overhung with long-armed pines, riding along the edge of a small, clear stream. Zeke edged along, no longer fighting to outpace a car.

"This'll take us to another road a little ways up," he said over his shoulder. "You all right?"

"Yes."

And she had been until that moment. Suddenly, it all sunk in with a strangely twisted, surrealistic quality. She—Mattie O'Neal, until lately a simple secretary in the English department of a small Midwestern university—was now riding through primeval forestland with some wild stranger, running away from two desperate men who had shot at her. Impossible.

But she was. The lurking memories of the night that had sent her running in the first place now flooded back, triggered by the sound of gunfire and the terror she'd felt both times. A thick trembling rocked her body, uncontrollable.

Zeke stopped the bike and got off, gathering her into a sturdy embrace. "You'll be all right, honey." He rubbed her arms, her back, firmly. "Take a few deep breaths and get a drink from the stream. I don't want to hang around long."

She nodded and he let her go, taking a canteen from a hook under the seat. He knelt at the edge of the stream to fill it and Mattie stared at him, still uncomprehending. "How—"

"Come on, Miss Mary," he said. "Don't fall apart on me now."

She gave herself a mental shake, shoving away the gruesome memories and the terror. Kneeling by the stream, she splashed her face and took a long, calming drink. "I'm ready."

He gave her a nod and fired up the bike.

It never occurred to Mattie to ask where they were going. Away. That was what mattered. They were going away from Brian.

Shock cocooned Mattie. The stark, harshly beautiful landscape of the northern Arizona plateau and the constant sound of the bike's engine numbed her. She gave herself up to the hypnotic sound of the wind, the gritty feel of it on her skin. Vaguely, she was aware of the heat of the sun on her arms, of Zeke in front of her, piloting her escape, of the curious faces of children as they passed.

In the early afternoon, they stopped at a roadside café in the mountains of New Mexico. Mattie stared at the menu without comprehension. Apparently sensing her confusion, he ordered burritos and coffee for both of them. Mattie ate hers dutifully. She couldn't think of anything to say that wouldn't lead back to the horrifying image of bullets flying around them, so she didn't talk. Zeke didn't seem to mind. They got back on the road quickly.

At sunset, they pulled into a small mountain town in Colorado. Pagosa Springs, the sign said.

The air cooled sharply, and the sudden drop in temperature roused Mattie from her stupor. Zeke drove slowly through the small town, and roused, Mattie looked around curiously. Children played hide-and-seek in some bushes. Through screen doors, supper light fell to porches, welcoming and soft. A dog ran behind a boy on a bike.

Zeke pulled into a hamburger stand, not a chain, but a mom-and-pop joint with broad windows all around. Old-fashioned. On the door, a fading sign in the colors of the old drive-in movie snack announcements advertised double-chocolate malts and curly fries. Two teenagers occupied a booth by the window, and a young mother with three little children had another. As Mattie watched, a burly man in a sheriff's uniform paused beside the woman's table to chat.

Zeke swore mildly. "I was going to suggest we go in and eat, but maybe it would be better if you stay out of sight."

"Why?"

He gracefully slid from the bike and yanked the helmet from his head. Hair fell down around his shoulders, mussed and yet gloriously sexy. A fist hit her belly at the pure animal beauty of him. "It's a long story, but if I recognized you, someone else who's a little bit faster on the uptake might recognize you, too. Just sit tight. I'll get us something to eat."

In his voice was the same careful tone he'd used with her all day. This time, Mattie found it annoying. "I'm not going to break, Zeke."

His grin was swift and dazzling. Mattie blinked.

"I knew you'd snap out of it," he said. Setting the helmet on the seat in front of her, he asked, "They make great hamburgers here. You want one?"

"Sure. With cheese." She pursed her lips and pointed toward the faded sign on the door. "And one of those super-duper chocolate malts, too."

He continued grinning at her as if she'd done something extraordinary. "No problem. I'll be right back. Keep your helmet on."

She watched him, moving with loose-limbed grace on long legs, and thought of JRR Tolkien's Strider. It would be a good nickname for him.

The thought made her grin. Strider had been quite a hero, after all. She doubted Zeke thought he'd done anything heroic today, but he had.

He'd saved her life.

Chapter 6

Carrying bags of food into a little motel on top of a hill, Mattie and Zeke sprawled on the two double beds in the room. "Your malt, *madame*," Zeke said. "Your cheeseburger. Fries." He reached deeper into the bag. "Ketchup, pickles, salt."

Mattie grinned. "What a guy. But that would be *mademoiselle,* not *madame.*"

"Give it back, then."

"You'd have to kill me first," she said. "I'm about to starve." She bit into the thick, greasy burger. Heaven.

"Me, too. Riding in the open air will definitely give you an appetite."

Her head, after wearing the helmet all day, felt extraordinarily light. "My head feels like it did after I cut my hair."

Zeke looked up, raising an eyebrow. "That was why I couldn't figure out who you were—your hair. On

TV, they showed a picture of you with it long. Real long."

"TV?"

"Yep. You were a featured story on that mysteries program a week or two ago." He dipped fries in ketchup, lovingly. "That's what was driving me so crazy. I *knew* I'd seen your face and that it was important. It was on television."

Her heart squeezed. "You're kidding."

"Wish I was. That's why you have to keep yourself scarce. The police in Kansas City have a reward out for any information leading to the arrest and conviction of some guy in Kansas City. You're wanted for questioning in connection with the murder of three men in a trucking warehouse."

Mattie felt faint. The reward was no doubt for Brian. "I wonder how they knew to look for me." An image of the night that had sent her running tried to surface, but Mattie wasn't ready for it yet. "How much is the reward?"

"Twenty-five thousand dollars." Zeke squeezed another ketchup packet onto the hamburger wrapper he was using as a plate. "He's a big-time bad boy."

Mattie closed her eyes. "He'll kill me if I go back there."

"Who is he, Mattie?" Zeke waited, hamburger in hand, for her answer. "He described your hair, too."

"It was the only thing that stood out about me." A tinge of bitterness ached in her. Now Brian would know her hair was gone. Cutting it had all been for nothing. Putting her hamburger aside, she wiped her fingers on a paper napkin and opened her heavy leather purse. At the bottom, coiled like a silky snake, was her braid. She pulled it out.

It unfurled from her hand to swing between them, a golden brown rope nearly three feet long. "It might be kind of sick to keep it," she said, "but I couldn't bring myself to throw it away."

Without speaking, Zeke touched it with one long finger. An odd expression crossed his face. He looked up. "You must have been really scared, to cut off that much hair."

"I was. I am." She coiled the braid around her wrist, remembering the feel of it swishing over her back, brushing her hips. Cloaking her. "But I didn't have a choice."

"You're a brave little mouse, Miss Mary," he said, and there was a rumbling, almost painfully seductive note to his voice. "You seem so vulnerable, but you've done what you had to do. I don't believe I've ever met a woman quite like you."

She touched the quivering leap in her belly, but couldn't tear her gaze from the green waters of his eyes. Something flickered there, warm and approving. She felt herself flush and hurriedly lowered her head. "Not too many women carry around a braid, that's for sure."

"That wasn't what I meant."

"I know." She picked up her hamburger. "Who was with him this morning?"

"I guess the redhead is the one you're running from?"

"Brian Murphy. And I'd guess it was Vincent Paglio with him. A dark man with a pockmarked face?"

"That's the one." He narrowed his eyes. "Who are they?"

"What did they say on TV?" she countered, unwilling to say more than she had to.

"I don't remember," he said with a hard edge.

Mattie glanced up in surprise. His mouth was set in sharp lines, and his eyes had gone very, very cold. Suddenly, she wondered if she'd gone from the frying pan into the fire. "I didn't ask for your help," she said, wounded by his icy expression.

"That's true," he said. "I guess you'd rather be a Jane Doe at the county coroner's office right now, huh?"

The terror of that bullet-riddled ride down the highway flooded back. "No," she said. "I didn't mean that."

"Well, then, why don't we get this story out of the way? No tricks, honey. I've been burned before and I wouldn't take kindly to having it happen again."

Carefully, she set aside her food and tucked her feet under her legs. She took a deep breath and opened the locked box in her mind. "Brian Murphy was my fiancé," she said at last. "He used me as an alibi so he could kill three men. Or rather, he tried to use me as an alibi."

Zeke waited.

Mattie went on, her words emotionless as she tried to keep her memories from overwhelming her. "He'd taken me out to dinner and we stopped at a party afterward. Something happened there, something that made him really angry. He made a couple of phone calls—one of them to Vince."

She closed her eyes. "I should have stayed at the party."

Silently, Zeke handed her the milk shake. She took a sip and gave him a brief history of the trucking firm and Brian's successful bid to bring it back from the brink of ruin. "I know now that he was transporting something illegal—but I didn't know that then."

"Drugs and guns," Zeke said. "The guns are the big problem. The police found a truckload of AK47s in the warehouse."

Guns. Mattie thought of the strife tearing cities—including Kansas City—to pieces. "He used to talk about the gun problem like he really cared," she said, and felt betrayed and stupid all over again.

"Makes a nice smoke screen, right?"

Mattie nodded cynically. "Anyway, that night he drove us over to the warehouse, said he just needed to check something and we'd go to my house. We went in and he made a couple more phone calls. I could tell he was just furious about some kind of shipment that had been waylaid."

She had begun to feel uneasy by then. The warehouse was dark and shadowy and felt somehow threatening. Dressed in a taffeta gown and high heels, Mattie didn't want to sit down anywhere, so she paced the small office as Brian made his phone calls.

"It started to bother me, that he wouldn't say what was going on and that he was so angry. It was almost like he was afraid."

Three other men had shown up at the warehouse, men Mattie didn't like. "Brian told me to drive his car to my house and he'd have someone give him a ride there in the morning to pick it up. I was tired and a little annoyed, so I did."

"You would have been his alibi," Zeke said.

"Exactly." A hundred times, a thousand, she'd wondered what would have happened if she'd made it home. "I got almost all the way to my apartment before I realized I'd forgotten my purse, which had all my keys in it. I had to go back."

Her mouth dried and she crossed her arms over her chest. "I could hear an argument when I got to the door, so I slipped to one side, behind a truck. I was just going to be inconspicuous, get my purse and get out of there."

She started to tremble and hugged herself closer. "I got to the office, grabbed my purse and was on my way out when Brian—um—" Her voice shook. She pressed her lips together and took a breath. "When he started shooting. I heard it before I saw it—there was so much noise—it echoed all through the room. It was huge, there were so many bullets..."

Blood everywhere. One of the men slammed against the truck she was hiding behind and he fell, his life spilling out on the floor all around. "I was frozen, kind of. I couldn't think what to do. He fell right by my foot and blood got on my shoe."

She stared at the floor, seeing in memory the traumatic moment. She gestured toward the mess she could see. "It was just everywhere. I'd never seen anyone shot except in the movies. I couldn't believe how much one person could bleed."

"Mattie."

She ignored him. "I looked up and Brain was standing there with this enormous gun and there was this look on his face—I knew he was going to kill me, too. So I ran."

Zeke moved abruptly, came to sit next to her. He took her hand. "You don't have to tell me any more. I'm sorry—"

"I slipped," she said in the same dull voice. The shivering in her limbs grew nearly uncontrollable.

Distantly, she felt Zeke's strong arms encircle her, warm and steady, but she couldn't stop the unreeling filmstrip. "I fell," she said. "Right in that man's blood. It got all over me. My knee. My hand. But I couldn't stop. I ran out and stole Brian's car. I just started driving."

"I'm sorry, Mattie," Zeke said again, and tucked her head into his shoulder. "I shouldn't have asked."

"I don't know how he found me," she said. "I don't know how the police knew I was there."

"You probably left prints at the scene."

"My hands—" she held them up "—got bloody."

He caught her hands in his own. "I'm sorry, Mattie."

The trembling eased a little as she absorbed his strength and warmth. "But how did Brian find out I was in Kismet?" she said, lifting her head. "I'd never been there before. Never even heard of it before I got on the bus."

"It isn't as hard as you might think to track someone. You must have dumped the car, right?"

She nodded, feeling calm enough to pull away from him before she made a fool of herself.

"He started there, I can tell you." He let her go. "It's the police looking for you, Mattie, not him. They said on that program that they've been trying to put him away for years, but hadn't had anything solid to go on." He cleared his throat. "The men he killed were undercover detectives. They almost had him."

"I thought you said you didn't remember the program."

"I wanted to hear your side."

"Wanted to make sure I told the truth."

He was unapologetic. "Yeah."

Mattie nodded.

"Why don't you just turn yourself in? It would be the easiest way—and you'd be doing a good deed."

"No." The word was flat and harsh. "He might not be able to kill me himself, but he'd find someone to do it."

"If his house of cards is collapsing—and it sounds like it is—he won't have the power to do that."

"No."

He shrugged. "Suit yourself."

She sighed, suddenly exhausted by the whole day. "I will."

"How did you get mixed up with someone like that?"

"I didn't know he was like that until that night. I met him at Mass. He used to bring his mother."

"Mass?"

"Yes. He seemed like a good Irish Catholic guy. He had a big family, a successful business. I really thought . . ." She trailed off.

"Thought what?"

"That I was finally going to have a family of my own," she said quietly. "Losing that dream was almost worse than anything else."

"I understand that," Zeke said. "More than you know."

She looked at him intently, curious at the sound of old pain in his words. His expression was so bitter, she decided not to breach it. She shifted and groaned at the pull of muscles in her body. All over her body. "I had no idea riding a motorcycle was so much work," she said ruefully.

"You're likely to be pretty sore in the morning. Why don't you go take a hot shower?"

Mattie nodded. She was so tired, she could sleep sitting up, right there on the edge of the bed. Without another word, she grabbed her tote bag and headed for the bathroom.

Zeke let out a breath as the shower kicked on in the other room. Maybe he could pull himself together before she came out.

Again he told himself good girls just weren't his speed. Especially good girls who went to Mass on Sunday mornings. No, he corrected himself, not a girl. A woman who went to Mass. A woman with quiet allure instead of flashy charms. He liked fast women because he was a fast, blunt man.

But his body didn't seem to be getting the message. He'd spent the day with her soft breasts pressed gently against his back, with her thighs cradling his hips, her arms wrapped around his waist.

Even now, the memory had his unrepentant parts jumping in anticipation. He shifted irritably.

He was the one who needed a shower. A nice, sharp, cold one.

The situation was not improved when she emerged, her hair combed wet around her gamine face. Her skin held a dewy, scrubbed freshness, and she wore the baggy tank top and dowdy shorts he'd seen the morning at the canyon.

Except now, she wore no bra, and her breasts swayed seductively as she moved, bumping the cloth over them subtly. Subtle. Everything about her was subtle, hidden to those who didn't take the time to look: her sable-colored hair and soft brown eyes, that fragile collarbone and long, graceful neck.

"You're too little for all that hair," he said suddenly. "Nobody would see you at all."

She touched her neck and Zeke wanted to touch it, too, with his hands and lips and tongue. Wanted to taste her throat and those plump, perfect lips. A tic jumped in his eye.

"It was my only real beauty," she said, smiling ruefully. "One of my foster mothers used to tell me that a lot. That my hair was my glory."

That foster mother needed her head examined, he thought, and touched with his gaze the crook of neck and shoulder that seemed to beg for a kiss.

Damn. How was he going to get from the bed to the shower without showing off all his own charms at full alert? He'd been grateful for the two beds, but hadn't anticipated this part…being with her in a close, quiet room, having to smell her scent of soap and freshness.

His quandary was solved when she flipped back the covers and climbed into bed. "I hope you don't mind," she said, her eyes already closing. "I'm beat."

"Not at all." Tenderness gentled his desire as she nestled close into the pillows. She was asleep in seconds.

Leaving him alone to grapple with the fact that once again, he'd stuck his nose in someplace where it didn't belong. His weakness for the small and defenseless was going to get him in trouble one of these day. Big trouble.

In fact, this situation seemed to smack of big trouble. Old Brian sounded like the worst kind of man—mean and desperate. Like Mattie, Zeke had no doubts she'd be dead if Brian found her.

He hadn't been thinking this morning, not about long-term consequences. He'd operated on pure instinct, first to snatch her from her cabin, then in heading this direction. Now he wondered how wise it was. Until now, the land he owned in these mountains had been sacrosanct, his alone. He'd never been there with anyone—it was another of his rules. It was his own private retreat, the only thing he'd managed to save when his life had fallen apart two years ago.

But there was no place else. On his land, Mattie would be safe until they could figure out a long-term solution to her problem.

Wearily, he stood up, kicked off his boots, stripped off his shirt and headed for the shower. Her voice stopped him. "Zeke?"

He turned, cursing himself and feeling exposed. "Yeah?" Maybe the shadows and her sleepiness would cover him.

"You saved my life today."

A clutch of something touched his chest, deep inside. "No, Miss Mary, you'd have figured something out."

She turned on the bed. One full breast nearly spilled out of her shirt, but he was sure she didn't know it. He struggled to keep his eyes on her face, but that sweet curve nearly blinded him, right at the bottom of his peripheral vision. "He would have killed me," she said. "I wouldn't have had a chance to get away."

"You'd be surprised what you can do," he said gruffly, and escaped into the bathroom. Maybe by the time he finished his shower, she'd be asleep.

But she wasn't. In fact, she seemed to have caught a second wind, for she'd tossed off the covers and was leaning against the headboard, flipping channels lazily.

She seemed to have no earthly idea how appealing she was in her baggy shirt, with the loose shorts showing off her sexy legs. Wisps of hair had dried in wavelets around her waifish cheeks. His body, tamed to subservience for a moment, leaped to attention again, and he jumped into the bed, jeans and all, before she could realize it.

"Whatcha watching?" he asked.

A shrug. "News."

"You mind if I shut off the light?" He reached for it, giving her little choice, but he wasn't quite quick enough. Before he reached the switch, he saw her eyes snag on the scars that riddled his back and sides. There were some on his arms, too, but they didn't stand out so much there, where people naturally got cuts and scrapes and such.

He clicked off the light. "Good night, Mattie," he said. "Get some rest, huh?"

He felt her liquid gaze on him. He closed his eyes and covered his head with the pillow to shut her out.

"Zeke?"

He sighed. "Yeah?"

"Why are you doing this?"

"I don't know, Mattie," he said hoarsely. "Somebody has to help you."

"Well, I want you to know I'll be okay now. You don't have to be my bodyguard or anything like that. There's no reason for you to get mixed up in all this."

"I'm already mixed up in it," he said, shoving the pillow into better shape.

"Tomorrow, I'll hitch a ride somewhere, or something. You can go back home."

"Kismet isn't home."

"Whatever." She sighed. "I just don't want to burden you. It's my problem and I'll solve it."

"Not alone you won't."

"I just wanted you to know," she said, and he heard the rustle of covers settling. He pushed away the tempting visions his mind offered and tried to get some sleep. Tried not to think of her sweet curves, all warm and fresh, only a few feet away.

He had to be crazy.

Scars.

His back and sides and stomach were littered with them. In the still light of morning, Mattie could see there were some of the same marks on his arms, but they passed unnoticed until you saw the same pattern on the rest of him. She sat on the side of her bed, already dressed, her hands folded, and absorbed them.

Tiny half moons and jagged little Z's. A couple of long, long stripes that looked like the marks of a whipping. A single jagged, puckered scar, shaped like a crescent, looked as if it had healed poorly. The worst were the cigarette burns. Unmistakable if you'd ever seen them, and Mattie had.

Upon closer examination, she saw a small scar by his eye, one thin mark on his mouth. All of them were very old, healed a long, long time ago.

She sighed. It had been a long time since she'd seen this kind of damage. Jamie had some of the same kinds of marks—and undoubtedly Zeke's had come from the same source. It made her feel a little sick.

As she watched him sleep, the sun suddenly burst between the cracks in the curtain to gild him, hiding the marks of a brutal childhood, and Mattie heard a tiny pained sound of surprise escape her throat. It was one thing to allow herself to see him as the grown man Jamie might have become if he'd survived. It was quite another to allow this wave of desire to fill her.

And yet, how could she help it? He was the most beautiful man she had ever seen.

Roxanne's words came back to her: *I want you to think about that man in your bed, with nothing on except maybe a sheet.*

Well, it wasn't her bed and he did wear a pair of jeans, but the rest was right. A thick restlessness crawled in her limbs, moved low in her belly. All the careful controls she'd exercised over herself disappeared like spiderwebs in a gust of wind. That fast, that completely.

She wanted him. Not in the sweet way of poetry, though there was that music in the symmetry of his body, in the careful meshing of bone and sinew and flesh that made him.

Her want was raw. Physical. She felt it in the palms of her hands and the flesh of her lips and the heaviness of her breasts.

In her life, she'd been hungry, and thirsty. She'd needed sleep. She had never, in her life, *needed* to touch a man.

Why this one? He was sexy, but he wasn't really her type. He hadn't been particularly nice to her aside, of course, from the fact that he'd saved her life. But this…lust or whatever it was, had started the day he'd walked into the café and electrified her with one long glance.

A flush touched her cheeks at the pagan nature of her thoughts, but even that didn't shame her enough to make her look away.

As if her examination were physical, he started awake. For a minute, he blinked uncertainly, obviously getting his bearings, then turned and saw Mattie. Staring at him.

For one long moment, she was snagged by his pale green eyes, so startling in his dark face. The expression in them grew from sleepy to amused. "'Mornin'" he said, the word slow and deep. He moved a little, settling his head more comfortably in the pillows. Mattie's blood danced.

"'Morning," she said, and hated herself for the soft, whispery sound of it.

"How long you been sittin' there?"

"I don't know."

He reached out unexpectedly and touched her calf. "Like what you see?"

To her surprise, Mattie didn't move away. Along his jaw was a shadow of beard, and his hand, moving lazily on her leg, was strangely stirring. The wild, raw need in her jumped another notch. He touched her ankle, his gaze on her face, moving all over it like a caress.

"I won't bite." He tugged a little on her leg. "Come on."

Panic struck her. Abruptly, she jumped up and moved away, putting her back to him. "I'm starving," she said. "I was about to wake you up so we could get something to eat."

"Is that what you were doing?"

"I don't know," she said honestly, and turned. It was a mistake. He'd shifted so he lay on his stomach, his head sideways on the pillow, his long, brown, muscled back displayed in full beauty. The sight of it struck her hard. Her breath left her on a little sigh.

"Don't," he said. The teasing fled his eyes. "It was all a long time ago."

The scars. "Zeke, that's not—"

His face was painfully wary and sharply shuttered. "Yeah," he said shortly, and got to his feet. "Tell me you didn't sit there feeling sorry for me, Miss Mary. Wondering how poor old Zeke got so messed up."

She pressed her lips together. "I didn't have to wonder," she said quietly. "I lived in a lot of foster homes. Most of them were okay, but there was a man in one of them who did that to some of the boys."

"Well, mine wasn't a foster parent. He was the real thing."

"Was?"

"He got beat to death in a bar fight when I was seventeen." He grabbed his shirt from the back of the chair and tugged it on. "It was the happiest day of my life."

Mattie said nothing.

He took his socks from his boots and grimaced. "It'll be nice to get some clean clothes on. I hate dirty socks." He put them on, anyway. "I'll run and get us some breakfast and we can get on the road again."

"No, Zeke."

"Thought you said you were hungry."

"Not no food, no more hiding. I can't stand to be in here like this, all cooped up. I'll wear your sunglasses if you think it's that big a deal." She had another agenda in mind, too, but she'd wait until he'd eaten something before she plunged into that. "I want to be outside."

He considered for a minute. "You still don't take it seriously, do you? You think you're in some movie and some good guy is going to come along at the right moment every so often."

That stung. "No, I just..." She shook her head. "I don't want to be stuck in this room when there's a whole beautiful little town out there to look at."

He chuckled. "You oughta see your eyes when you say that. I thought they quit making such sweet women a long time ago."

"Is that a yes?"

"I guess it is."

Chapter 7

Over big plates of pancakes and scrambled eggs, Mattie leaned forward. "Can I take off these glasses in here? I feel silly eating breakfast with sunglasses on."

"The waitress already heard your excuse. You've got a light-sensitivity problem." He grinned, rather wickedly, Mattie thought.

"But I can't see the view at all." She peeked over the top of the sunglasses to the stair-stepped expanse of blue mountains, drawn across the horizon like a jagged curtain. "I never dreamed there was anything so beautiful."

"It is beautiful," he said, and Mattie thought his eyes, soft with appreciation, ran a close second to the view. "I always think about it when I'm not here."

Mattie dipped her head, letting the glasses slide down her nose, to look at him. "You mean this was a destination? You drove here on purpose?"

Zeke chuckled. "Yep."

Nonplussed, she put down her fork. "Oh."

He went back to his pancakes. The waitress came by with more coffee and Zeke gave her a friendly smile. She smiled back. Naturally.

That single exchange—Zeke's effortless and omni-present charm and the waitress's immediate re-sponse—brought everything into focus for Mattie. She didn't know what his motives were, why he'd so self-lessly rescued her, but she couldn't let it go on. "Zeke," she said, "I appreciate everything you've done for me."

"Mmm." He swallowed. "I hear a 'but' in there."

"I can't let you do any more. If you'd be so kind as to take me to the bus station, I'll get out of your hair."

Carefully, he crossed his fork and knife on his empty plate and pulled his coffee cup forward. "How long do you think you'll last before old Brian tracks you down again?" He cocked his head. "Maybe next time you won't be lucky enough to be warned ahead of time."

"I'll dye my hair," she countered. "Get some weird glasses at Goodwill or something. It's not as hard as you think to become invisible."

His mouth twitched. "And you aren't nearly as in-visible as you think you are." He leaned forward, dropping his elbows on the table. "How are you gonna hide that long, pretty neck? That sexy mouth? That siren body of yours?"

Mattie had touched her neck when he mentioned it, but her cheeks flushed bright red at the last turn of phrase. "You don't have to get crude," she protested, lowering her eyes.

"That's a long way from crude, Miss Mary," he said with a scowl. "Believe me."

"Zeke," she said in a small voice, "you scare me. How do I know you aren't worse than what I'm running from?"

"You don't," He plucked the check from the table between them. "Not in any way that matters, in facts and figures. Guess you'll have to trust your instincts."

"What instincts?" she said scornfully. "The ones that led me to think a major criminal was just a nice Catholic fellow?"

Zeke stared at her, his face utterly expressionless. "Don't give me that look," she snapped. "Say something."

"What do you want me to say, Mattie? I'm not gonna try to prove myself to you."

Now she realized she'd wounded him the smallest bit. He probably had justification for feeling hurt, too, but that didn't change Mattie's uncertainty. She stared at him, struggling for clues to his true nature.

Her instincts. What had her instincts said about Brian Murphy? Hadn't there been moments of warning, moments his smile seemed forced? Dozens of times, hadn't she beaten back the screams of those instincts because she so desperately wanted what he seemed to offer?

And what did they tell her about Zeke? She bit the inside of her cheek, seeing a man who'd known a lot of pain. A man who could likely be violent if the need arose, but wouldn't be if he could avoid it. She saw the man who danced with a fussy baby to calm him and the man who'd rescued her without a moment's hesitation.

"I don't want to be a burden," she said at last. "You can't imagine how much I hate that."

"You couldn't be a burden if you tried." His mouth softened. "I couldn't live with myself if you went out there and got yourself killed."

Terrific, Mattie thought. A pity case. "Zeke—"

"Listen, Mattie." He covered her hand with his own. "I've been lost in my own problems for longer than I like to say. Let me help you."

She looked at his hand, at the long fingers and strong, sinewy lines. There was both strength and gentleness in that hand, just as there was in the man himself. "All right," she said. "Where are we going?"

He smiled. "I have some land up in the mountains. Cabin isn't fancy, but it keeps the rain off. We'll go there until we can figure out what comes next."

"Okay," she said. "I trust you."

His fingers curled around hers. "Let's go."

The day before, Mattie had been too numb with shock to appreciate the pleasures of riding on the back of a motorcycle. This morning, there was no such muffling.

They left town and headed up into the mountains, traveling on a normal blacktop highway, well maintained and obviously heavily traveled. After a while, Zeke turned onto a smaller, narrower road. They followed the strip of asphalt upward, over passes that hugged the sheer side of a cliff, the drop on one side thousands of feet. A delicious dizziness engulfed Mattie at the dangerous thrill of it, and she couldn't help gripping Zeke more closely. He chuckled at such times, a rumbling she felt through her fingers on his chest rather than heard through her ears.

They rode through little towns with names like Santa Ana and Kinnikinnik and Ute City, little more than scatterings of cabins and a shop or two along the state road. Here hunters bought permits, anglers picked up tackle, campers stocked up on beer and groceries they'd forgotten.

The *wilderness,* Mattie thought with a thrill of happiness. Just like Laura in the *Little House* books, she was striking out for adventure in a sparsely settled, wild place. A hundred years ago, there had been only mountain men and Indians and animals and silence. Zeke, she thought with some certainty, would have been among them. In any age, she had a hunch he'd be an outsider, a loner.

She inhaled deeply of the spice-scented mountain air, thin and cool in spite of the summer weather. She filled her eyes with the colors of the high country: the azure sky punctuated with arrows of deep green pine, the slender white trunks of aspen like bars of light in the dark forests, the misty dark blue of the distant mountainsides, falling away to purply black in the shadows of the valley. She liked the wind in her face, and immediacy of seeing it all without windows to blunt the view, and the deep growling purr of the bike itself.

Most of all, she liked the feeling of Zeke before her and the pleasure of being able to touch him freely without having to explain why—to him or to herself—it was so satisfying. She was careful to keep the clasp of her hand light, nonintrusive, careful not to press too much or too often into the temptation of his back. Businesslike, she held onto his sides, imagining a dance chaperon's hand placed between their bodies.

There was nothing she could do, no adjustment she could make, to keep her thighs from clasping the sides of his hips and legs. She tried not to make too much of it, but it was impossible not to feel it—those long hard thighs, the shift of muscle in his buttocks. Intimate and casual at once.

At midmorning, a sudden bank of clouds moved in over the valley. They filled the sky almost at once, as if some cosmic force had tossed a thick gray blanket over the sky. When the sun disappeared, the temperature dropped, and a chill wind sprung up. Mattie shivered.

"We're almost there," Zeke called over his shoulder. "We might get wet, but it won't be too bad."

"Okay!"

Just as the first light sprinkles began to spatter them—amazing how the speed of the bike made even such light spatters hurt—Zeke turned on to a narrow dirt track. Tire tracks showed where a truck had come through, over and over.

The path bumped and twisted through thick trees; potholes and rocks littered the way. Then, the rain began to fall in earnest.

"Sorry," Zeke called, fighting his way up the steep path. "I can't go any faster or we'll likely go flying."

"I'm all right," she returned and leaned closer into him for protection. Her shoulders and arms and back were getting soaked, but it wasn't an unpleasant experience. The rain released the smell of earth and spice inherent to the forest; it cascaded over the tree trunks and dripped in crystal drops from pine needles. Beautiful.

Also cold. When they pulled into a clearing, Mattie dismounted and ran with Zeke into a small, neat cabin, newly built, by the look of it. Details blurred in the steadfast rain.

"Whew," Zeke said, shaking himself off, closing the door behind her. "You never know when those storms'll hit until they're right up on you."

Mattie tugged off her helmet, dropped her bags by the door and took the towel he offered. "Brrr. Amazing how cold a summer rain can be!"

"Takes some getting used to, all right." He rubbed his long hair. "Rain is always cold in Colorado. Most of the time in the summer, there's so much lightning you don't want to be out in it anyway." Looping the towel around his neck, he asked, "You want some coffee?"

"Please."

He stepped outside for a minute, pot in hand, and Mattie assumed he had to get water from somewhere. She glanced around curiously. The cabin was a single large room with a fireplace at one end and a bed at the other. Between was a modern-looking stove, next to some open shelves, well stocked with supplies. A mishmash of cups, glasses and unmatched plates were neatly stacked on one, the others held pots and pans, canned goods and sturdy tin canisters.

Opposite the stove, below a window, sat a couch and a worn chair. Another floor-to-ceiling block of shelves held books, paperbacks, mostly. A double bed, covered with a sleeping bag, completed the picture.

The room smelled of new wood, and time had not yet darkened the yellow pine planks on the floor. The wooden, multipaned windows fit the rustic atmosphere, but they were new, no doubt ordered to fit. As Zeke returned, she asked, "Did you build this cabin?"

He lit the fire on the stove with a kitchen match and put the blue-and-white spatterware coffeepot on the fire. "Yeah," he said and rubbed more dampness from his face as he looked around. "Someday, this is supposed to be the living room, but for now, it's pretty much everything."

"Yourself?" she asked, touching the smooth pine wall. "You built it all?"

Zeke grinned and held up his big, lean hands. "All by my little lonesome."

"Amazing."

He took a can of coffee from the shelf and measured it into the pot. "My dad was a carpenter," he said, not looking at her. "He made sure I knew how to do it right."

The father again. Mattie collected the note to add to the others she held in her mind, but said nothing. Wandering over to admire a handcarved windowsill, she thought, *nice revenge*. "Pretty impressive," she said aloud.

"Well don't get too excited until you see the rest of the amenities," he drawled and gestured toward the back door. It led to a wide, covered porch, comfortable with benches and chairs.

Breathing deeply of the rainy air, Mattie sighed. "It never smells like this in the city."

He pointed. "On clear days, you can see clear to Montana from here."

Mattie looked out over the mist-shrouded landscape and saw hints of what he meant. "Are these the other amenities?"

"No." Nodding toward the left, he said, "They're over there. I do have the luxury of a crude shower, but it's open to the elements. That's a sauna in the bigger building. That one—" he pointed to an unmistakable hut on the other side of the clearing "—is just what it looks like."

Mattie laughed. "How perfect!"

"Perfect?"

"I love this, Zeke!" She turned to look up at him. "A real cabin in the mountains, with an outhouse and everything!"

A smile touched his sensual mouth, and a curious softness bloomed in his eyes. He lifted his hand, but it hovered between them uncertainly for a minute before landing on her shoulder. "You do have a way of looking at things, Miss Mary," he said, his voice low and rough.

She simply looked up at him for a moment, taking as deep and passionate a pleasure in the hard male power of his face as she had in the mountain views. For the first time in more than a month, she felt safe. "Thank you, Zeke."

His gaze shifted, flickered, and his fingers stirred restlessly against her neck. She thought he was going to kiss her, but he dropped his hand and straightened. "You're more than welcome, honey," he said gruffly. "Come on. That coffee should be about ready."

Mattie shot a glance toward the outhouse. It wasn't that she needed it so much as she just wanted to see what it looked like inside. "Um...do you mind if I go see what it looks like?"

His laugh was as full and natural as any she'd heard from him. "Go right ahead, Miss Mary. Go right ahead."

*   *   *

Zeke went inside to wait, a curious anticipation stirring in his belly. It was an odd emotion for him, and he paused in the middle of the room to try to identify it.

As a child, he'd fallen in love with the night sky, with the possibilities all those winking stars presented. He'd gulped astronomy from books out of the school library, then would check his new facts against the night. Staring up at that vast, unexplored universe, Zeke had found ways to keep going.

Mattie, with her eagerness and pleasure in each small thing she uncovered, made him feel the way that sky had. Made him remember what it was like to feel wonder. He felt the stirring in his belly again. More than wonder. There was hope mixed in there, too. How long since he'd felt either one?

A tiny explosion of warning popped in his brain. Hope was a dangerous emotion. Frowning, he took cups from the shelf and checked to make sure no weevils had infected the powdered cream. It was bad enough that he'd brought her here, breaking yet another of his rules. It would be sheer stupidity to get all gushy about the whole thing. She'd needed some help. Zeke gave it. No more than that.

Whatever it took, he had to keep her at arm's length.

But it was hard as hell. She sailed in, dewy-faced, her big doe eyes shimmering. "It's so amazing!" she exclaimed.

"Amazing. That's the third time you used that word in five minutes." His pleasure rolled from him on a laugh. "Did you check out the shower? Now, it's something."

"No. Sorry, I'll go back—"

He caught her arm. "I'll show it to you later. Come on and drink your coffee."

She shed her light jacket and sprawled out on the couch, mug in hand, looking around with an alert, interested gaze. "How can you have a shower and no toilet?"

"Toilets are more complicated to set up." He took the chair and kicked off his boots. "The shower is fed from the hot springs—so is the sauna."

"What's a hot spring?"

"You really are a city kid, aren't you?"

She nodded unapologetically, and bands of gray light flashed over the crown of her brown head. "I never even left Kansas City before I stole that car."

"Never?" Zeke thought of his wanderings. "Why?"

She lifted a shoulder. "There wasn't really ever money to go anywhere. I've been on my own since I was sixteen."

"No summer camp or vacations?"

"Did you go to summer camp and go on vacations, Zeke?" she asked quietly.

"No."

"Why not?"

He shrugged. "Money, I reckon."

"No poor child does those things."

He gave her a half smile. "Poor. I haven't heard anybody use that word in a long time, not in that way."

A twinkle shone in her eye. "Economically disadvantaged? Blue-collar?"

He laughed. "*Poor* works just fine." He drank from his cup, examining her more closely. She'd said she was a foster child, and he supposed that most homes that took such children in were not well-to-do, but she didn't have that air about her, even in the dowdy clothes she sometimes wore. "You don't look like that kind of a kid," he said with a frown.

"Is there a mark you look for?"

He pursed his lips, thinking of the trashy little houses back home, where hopeless women sat on rickety steps while their raggedy children wiped wrists over snotty noses. Wasn't like that in the city, he knew that, but there were things he noticed, things he'd grown sensitive to over the years. "Not one mark," he said. "A few of them. The way people talk, their teeth." He narrowed his eyes. "A certain posture, maybe."

"Like you?"

"What's that mean?"

"You don't have bad teeth, and heaven knows there's nothing submissive about your posture."

"My teeth are crooked."

"Only a little."

"But if I'd been a rich kid, they'd be straight, now, wouldn't they?"

"I suppose." Her sultry mouth tipped at the corners in a mischievous expression. "And your grammar could use some work."

"Hey, now," he warned, but chuckled in spite of himself.

"I think you're being narrow-minded."

He lifted his eyebrows ruefully. "Maybe."

She stretched comfortably, like a cat, and Zeke admired the generous curve of breasts the pose displayed before she curled up again, her gaze snagging on his books. "You must be a pretty serious reader."

Zeke shrugged. "No electricity. You learn to keep books around."

She chuckled, leaning over to read the titles. "I guess you've read *Black Beauty* and *King of the Wind* in recent months, then, huh?"

"Well, I guess there's a few there from when I was a kid." His books had been all he'd taken with him, but he'd spilled enough of his guts to this woman. He was dangerously close to letting down his guard.

"Looks like you were horse-crazy," she said, and looked up curiously. "Were you?"

Maybe he could admit that much. "Yeah." His gaze cut involuntarily toward the empty corrals and barn beyond the front window. Fences neat, ground smoothed, hay rotted to nothing in the stalls. Empty.

She followed his gaze and looked back at him, but didn't say anything. Rare quality in a woman, the ability to realize some things were off limits. She'd done the same thing over his scars—didn't duck from seeing them, but made a simple acknowledgment of them and what they were without a lot of melodrama or gnashing of teeth. "I always wanted to be a cowboy," he found himself volunteering. "Wear a bandanna around my neck and a big hat."

She smiled. "I wanted to be in the symphony."

"What did you play?"

The grin broadened. "Nothing. I just thought it would be fun to wear black velvet dresses and pearls and have a whole bunch of people in fancy clothes come listen to me."

Again he laughed, unable to help himself, and the odd wild emotion in his chest swelled again. "I wanted to wear spurs, so when I walked it would make noise."

"Looks like you got a little closer to your dream than I did mine," she said, pointing to the corrals.

He should have known it wouldn't slip by that easily. He stood up to pour another cup of coffee. "You hungry yet?"

"Not really. You don't have to do everything, you know. I'd be happy to cook. I'm very good at it." She materialized at his side, holding out her cup for a refill.

Zeke turned and poured, feeling her warmth along the length of his side. They stood in stocking feet, both of them, and she was small enough to tuck up under one arm. Wisps of hair curled around her small ears and the long, pretty neck and he knew an urge to bend close, touch his lips to that white throat. Curve a hand around her breast, another around that not-so-tiny bottom. She was little, but nothing had been spared on the curves. He liked that. "I've got a feeling, Miss Mary, that I'm gonna have some trouble keeping myself in line around you."

She lifted wide brown eyes to his face and he saw the stirring hunger there, the curious and frightened expression he'd first read on her face that day in the café. Her siren lips softened and he watched her gaze flicker over his face, touch on his lips, dart back to his eyes. "Maybe—"

"No way, sweetheart," he said gruffly, and put the pot on the stove, willing himself to look away from that hunger in her face. She'd fall in love. No way he could bear that—some long-twisted thing in his soul wasn't capable of accepting it. Just as soon as he thought he could, he'd end up stomping all over her.

"I told you before I'm not your kind of man. You don't need to get all torn up in addition to everything else that's going on in your life right now."

"You're a big, mean bear, all right," she said and he heard the amusement in her tone with surprise. "You think you are, Zeke, but you aren't."

"I mean it, Mattie," he said and faced her squarely. Come hell or high water, he found ways to drive women away once they proved themselves fool enough to fall in love with him. He liked Mattie too much as a friend to let that happen.

To emphasize his point, he put his coffee cup aside and settled his hands on her shoulders. Pretty, slim shoulders, fragile beneath his palms. "You're real vulnerable right now. Your fiancé betrayed you, you almost got killed and now you've had a little adventure."

She waited, her coffee cup between her palms, her eyes as calm as a summer morning. He could smell the faint scent of soap and motel shampoo around her, and felt the heat of her skin against his hands.

"Once you get back to normal life, you'll wonder what the hell you could have been thinking."

"Will I?" Her voice held a seductive, whispery note.

Zeke forgot what he meant to say, falling adrift in the seductively gentle liquid of her eyes. In their depths he saw something of himself, but stronger, all the things he might have been if only he'd had one person—

He kissed her before he knew he would do it. Cupped her small head against his hand and bent to touch her lips with his own, lightly tasting that sensuous mouth. He closed his eyes to feel it better—the moist plumpness of unseasoned lips, flavored with coffee and sugar and something that belonged only to her. And like an exhausted man sinking with gratitude into the down of a pillow, he sank into the softness, losing himself as he explored the edges and corners, the sensitive inner edge. He suckled gently and heard her sigh as she inclined her head to take him more fully.

A kiss. It was only a kiss. But he couldn't seem to surface, couldn't remember what urgent reason he had for not doing it. When she parted her lips, ever so slightly, he opened his mouth and found her tongue ready to dance with his own.

And it was right, by damn. The taste of her and the easy mesh of their ways, the fit of his lips against hers and the mingling of their tongues. He held her loosely, and kissed her. And kissed her. And once again.

A booming crack of thunder shattered the moment and Zeke jerked away. Her eyes had gone sultry, the hungriness in them a notch higher, a hunger reflected in the labored sound of his breath in his ears. "That wasn't—"

He swore. It had been a mistake to bring her here. No way on God's green earth he could resist her for days on end. No way.

He gritted his teeth. "I've got rules, Mattie. It's the only way I can keep things even. One of those rules is that I don't mess with good girls like you." He shook his head. "It just isn't a good idea for us."

She nodded, her eyes wide and sad. "I understand."

"I want you," he said, and there was relief in putting it into words. "But it would be wrong."

"Okay."

He backed away, unable to manage the simple acceptance in her face and what that told him about her. Life had taught her not to want things she couldn't have.

Hating himself, he grabbed the door handle. "I've got some things to take care of outside. Make yourself at home."

He fled, into the rain.

Chapter 8

Mattie watched him go. Left alone in the cabin, she stirred sugar carefully into her cup and sipped the painfully hot coffee, trying to burn away the trembling need he'd awakened in her. Everything shook with an infinitesimal trembling she couldn't control, didn't understand. Her spine felt like rubber, her limbs like cooked spaghetti. Elsewhere, in her breasts and low in her belly and in dark places she'd rarely named, he'd awakened a deep ache. Her skin felt too sensitive, irritated by the cloth over it. She pressed a palm against her chest, trying to ease the feeling.

Turning, she saw Zeke through the window, heedlessly striding on those long legs through the rain and lightning, his hair darkening as it got wet, the shoulders of his white shirt soaked and showing the skin beneath. Her only comfort was that he obviously needed to work off the same restless burning that consumed her.

I want you.

As she watched, he picked up a fist-size rock and pitched it hard. It landed on the roof of the stable.

Mattie sighed. It could get a bit tense if this was what they had to face while they were here.

Then again, maybe both of them were just reacting to the intensity of the past twenty-four hours. Now it was raining, which to Mattie always seemed an emotional sort of weather. Once the sun came out, it would be easier.

A little desire was natural under the circumstances. He worried a little too much about her fragility, but if it kept him at arm's length, maybe that was for the best. The kinds of things he stirred in her were probably better left unexamined.

He had warned her that once she got her life back together, she would wonder what she'd ever seen in him. The truth was, she had no idea who he was, really. Not intellectually. She reacted to him in purely instinctive ways, trusting him not because of what she knew, but what she felt to be true.

What if her instincts were wrong?

Absently, she touched the spines of his books. This was not the collection of a casual reader, whatever he wanted her to believe. The well-read volumes covered the childhood favorites she'd teased him about, but also included classics by writers such as Shakespeare and Dante and Dickens. One whole shelf was devoted to philosophy, and another held thrillers and mysteries. Spencer was a favorite, which somehow didn't surprise her. She pulled one book out at random and flipped through the pages.

But they didn't hold her attention. Again and again, her gaze was drawn to the man beyond the window. A man who seemed to have no job, but had managed to buy land and build a cabin on it. A man who rode a motorcycle and had a tattoo and wore to-hell-with-you hair, but read Shakespeare and Plato. A man with scars that suggested a kind of brutality most ordinary people could barely admit existed.

Secret sorrows of all sorts lurked in those pale green eyes. Mattie wanted to free them, let them out of the darkness where they moldered and into the sun, where they'd die a natural death.

But she knew even as she thought it, the wish was futile. If ever a man had built walls, Zeke had. She knew herself well enough to know she didn't have the kind of tools she needed to knock the walls down.

With a sigh, she put the book back and set about making something for their dinner. The least she could do was make herself useful.

Dinner was a quiet affair. Mattie had managed to put together a fairly decent offering of soup and canned fruit and crackers, and they ate it silently before the fire Zeke built.

She hadn't thought it was possible to be in the same room with someone for hours on end without speaking, but she'd never had to deal with a brooding man like Zeke before, either. Even when supper was finished and they'd cleaned up the dishes, he disappeared outside and didn't come back for quite a while, then making no comment or apology for it.

She tried to amuse herself with a novel, but reading seemed too tame. The rain fell steadily outside, making her restless. Annoyed with Zeke for his silly brooding, restless with nothing to do, she took an oversize jacket from a hook by the door and stepped out to the porch. Steaming cup of coffee in hand, she settled in one of the chairs and gazed out at the night.

The clouds had moved off, leaving behind a breathlessly black night. All the overused, overworked metaphors applied: it looked like black velvet studded with diamonds; like a movie star's dress; like magic and sequins and hope.

An ease passed through her. The silence was unbroken by even the scurry of animals or the call of a bird. The wind whispered, water trickled from some high place, and dripped into an unseen pool.

She smiled to herself. Kansas City, with its traffic and noise and thick air seemed a million miles away, and she was glad of it. All her life, she'd dreamed of places like this. She'd read of the English countryside or quiet groves in the mountains, or wilderness retreats, and a soft bloom of curious longing would fill her. To sit in silence like that!

And here she was, after the strangest series of events she could imagine. A month ago, she'd been planning her wedding.

That woman, the one who'd spent her days typing memos to department heads, her evenings tracing Byronic influences in Regency era poetry, and her weekends choosing silver patterns, seemed like a stranger. What Mattie saw about herself when she looked back from this vantage point was that she'd been sound asleep. Not living at all, just going through the motions.

She sipped her sweet, hot coffee. Brian. Why was it so easy to see now what she should have seen then? She had never been in love with him. He'd dazzled her and charmed her; they had a good time when they went places, shared a common interest in some things.

What she saw in retrospect was that their dealings with each other had always been unfailingly polite. Even the few times they'd actually made love had been neat and orderly, with the proper preparations and the lights turned low. Even the right music on in the background.

Mattie bit her lip. It was Zeke that made her old life seem so vapid. It was as if she'd been walking around in a black-and-white world until he walked into the café that morning and shown her Technicolor. The sound track of her old life was a careful minuet. Zeke brought with him some roaring, loud rock and roll.

How could a person ever go back?

She wouldn't. Whatever happened after all of this, she wouldn't return to Kansas City. The sleepwalker had awakened, and as painful as it had been to cut her hair, the symbolic shearing away somehow made her feel freer to choose a new life when—

When what? When Brian was safely in jail? Maybe. When this was all over. That was as much as she could manage for now.

A light shone in the darkness—a flashlight Zeke carried from the small shed he said contained a sauna. He took his time, the ease of his attitude evident in the lazy, long-legged way he crossed the clearing. "Hey, Strider," she said when he gained the porch steps.

"Strider?"

"Lord of the Rings," she said. "Surely you've read Tolkien."

He clicked off the flashlight and smiled. "Sure."

Seeing that smile, Mattie felt her breath leave her on a sigh of relief. "Does the sauna always improve your mood that much?"

"I reckon it does."

"You might have invited your guest along," she said lightly.

"Sorry, Miss Mary," he drawled. "But it was you I had to get away from."

The words stung, though she tried not to let them. "I didn't ask to come here," she said quietly. "You insisted."

"I know, and I don't regret it." He leaned on the rail nearby her; she could feel his extraordinary warmth along her knee. "But the whole point is to keep you safe until we figure out what to do, and the way I was feeling this afternoon wasn't going to get that done. You understand?"

She glared at him through the darkness. "I'm not nearly as fragile as you think I am, Zeke."

He shook his head, and reached into his shirt pocket for a cigarette. "I never said you were fragile. Matter of fact, I think you're damned brave." He bent over his lighter and a flare of orange cast deep shadows over the angles of his face. "You're also a good girl and I'm willing to respect that."

He had so dazzled her at first, she'd been unable to respond to these comments in the past. "I'm not a girl," she said, standing. "And I almost out-hustled you at pool, so I can't be that sweet."

"I don't mean anything bad by it, Miss Mary," he said, and there was amusement in his voice. "You're honest and nice and trustworthy."

She cocked her head. "Does that mean you're mean and crooked and untrustworthy?"

"Maybe."

"Then what the hell am I doing here at all?"

He laughed. "Okay, sometimes I'm a good guy."

"And sometimes," she said with narrowed eyes, "I'm not such a nice girl."

"Don't tempt me," he said, going still. "Me on a good day and you on a bad one still adds up to a bear and a mouse."

The growl in those words, the danger in that promise finally brought her to her senses. "You're right," she said. "If we're through parrying, I'd like to get some sleep."

He insisted she take the bed. He'd make a pallet on the floor. Mattie protested, vehemently. And Zeke steadfastly ignored her.

It panicked her just a little. She didn't want to sleep in his bed, on his pillow, with the smell of him, the imprint of his body all around her, when he'd made it very, very plain there would be nothing between them. It would drive her crazy.

But she lost the fight. He was simply, calmly, cheerfully immovable. She picked up the sleeping bag and threw it at him. "Fine, then," she said, taking pleasure in the solid thunk of the bag against his head.

He laughed. "Chill out, girl."

"Woman," she muttered, turning back to the bed. Under where the sleeping bag had been was a thick blanket, printed with horses. She chuckled, touching a rearing stallion that had obviously provided the model for his tattoo. "Sure you don't want your horse blankie?" she asked over her shoulder.

He was tugging off his boots, but spared a grin in her direction. "It was a present." The way he said it, she knew it was a woman. Some other woman that had lost out in the struggle for Zeke Shephard's heart.

There were probably dozens of them, Mattie thought with a scowl, shedding her own shoes.

"Which came first, the tattoo or the blanket?"

"Tattoo. I got it when I was fifteen. Got drunk with my friends and went into Jackson. One of the many times I ran away from home." He spread the couch cushions on the braided rug in front of the fireplace and shook the sleeping bag out over it. "Lasted two months, that time, though."

Mattie sat on the bed, watching him. Firelight caught in the waves of his hair as he unbuttoned his shirt. "You want to give me a minute of privacy here, Miss Mary? I'm not gonna make a habit of sleeping in my jeans."

Dutifully, she turned away, only now becoming aware of the intimacy of these surroundings when it came to things like dressing and undressing. She could wear her tank top and jeans to bed, she supposed, but getting in and out of them might prove a bit troublesome.

She heard a rustle, the clink of something in his pockets as his jeans hit the floor. "All right," he said after another minute. "I'm decent."

Mattie turned back to find him safely ensconced in the sleeping bag before the fire, his chest bare, his arms comfortably tucked under his head. A bright shock of need rippled through her—and the hunger was back, wild and hot.

Irritably, she dug through her tote and dragged out her tank top and shorts. For an instant, she considered slipping outside to change, but it was too cold. "Now if you'll afford me some privacy, Mr. Shephard?"

It was his turn to shift. Hastily, Mattie shed her jeans, all too aware of the sound the zipper made as it slid down, and shimmied into her shorts. Turning her back to Zeke, she yanked off her T-shirt, shivering a little at the wash of cool air on her skin. For one long, agonizing minute, she wondered if she ought to keep her bra on, just for the sake of modesty, but it would be miserably uncomfortable. What woman didn't take off a bra with a sigh of relief at the end of a day?

It felt as if it took forever, felt as if it took her a hundred minutes to undo the clasp, another fifty to slip it from her shoulders and discard it, another four hundred years that she stood there naked to the waist with a half-naked Zeke behind her. She peeked over her shoulder.

He had shifted to the way he was before, his hands clasped behind his head, the green eyes glittering with something dangerous and dark. Lazily, he smiled. "Told you I'm no nice guy."

Mattie clasped her arms over her breasts and glared at him. "Turn over right now or I swear I'll—"

He lifted up on one elbow, his pagan hair falling around his smoothly rounded shoulders, his expression even darker. "Or you'll what?"

She spun around and grabbed her shirt, her spine rippling with the caress of his eyes. With a yank, she tugged the shirt over her head and turned around. "You're a real son of a bitch," she said.

"Miss Mary!" he said mockingly. "I had no idea you could talk like that."

Furiously, she picked up her clothes, bending to retrieve her jeans and stuff them into the tote. "If the shoe fits..."

"I told you," he said, the teasing dropping away. "I told you."

"So you did." She scrambled under the horse blanket and leaned over to blow out the candle. "Good night, Zeke."

His voice was a slow, dark drawl. "'Night, Miss Mary."

Zeke woke just before dawn to a chorus of bird song. He heard the birds before he opened his eyes and knew instantly where he was.

Home.

Slowly, he stretched in his cocoon of a sleeping bag, feeling the deep relaxed pull of his muscles after a good sauna and a good night's sleep.

As was his habit here, he opened his eyes and looked around slowly, thankful for each tiny thing illuminated by the gold bar of early-morning sun that broke through the windows. Grateful for the pine walls and floor, for the good propane stove in the corner, for the fireplace that had given him such fits as he built it, but that now worked like a dream. Yeah, whatever they took, this was home. He left it often, but always came back.

From his vantage point on the floor, all he could see was the top of Mattie's glossy head, pointing at him at an angle. A spray of hair fanned over the edge of the mattress. A restless sleeper.

Quietly, so as not to disturb her, he got up and slipped into his jeans, got a clean shirt from the shelf and slipped outside to greet the morning.

And what a morning! Across the valley, washed sparklingly clean by yesterday's rain, he saw the first rays of dawn strike the distant blue mountainsides, throwing into mystic shadow the valleys and hidden crevices. Closer in, the tops of aspens rustled as if in greeting and arrows of sunlight kissed the uppermost leaves with a blaze of color. He inhaled deeply, smelling damp earth and pine needles and the crisp undernote of the mountains themselves. Glorious.

A tiny cracking branch drew his attention, and from the trees ambled a doe and her fawn, the fawn dancing to catch up. Upwind from him, the doe didn't sense Zeke's presence, and calmly nibbled leaves from a shrub.

Mattie had to see this. Walking backward slowly, he turned the door handle without a sound and eased inside. She hadn't stirred. She sprawled over the bed, corner to corner, the posture of a sleeper who had nothing to fear. He was glad of that, at least.

He touched her shoulder. "Mattie," he said in a deep whisper. "There's something you should see."

She roused instantly and blinked up. "What?"

"Be very quiet and come with me."

She got up and he took her hand, putting a finger to his lips, showing her how to move silently. They slipped out the door. She looked bewildered at first, but he drew her close and pointed over her shoulder to the feeding doe.

Her nearness unsettled him, but he didn't push her away, only watched the wonder dawn in those big eyes, watched the joy break on her face. They stood there for a long time, utterly still, his hands on her shoulders, until the deer tired of the spot and wandered into the trees.

When the last shadows of the deer were out of sight, she sighed and leaned into him. Zeke stiffened momentarily, but the fit of her head beneath his shoulder was too perfect to resist. He left his hands on her fragile shoulders, too, let them just rest there without moving. They didn't talk. Mattie simply leaned on him and he just as simply braced her, moving his chin on her hair as they took in the grandeur of the mountain morning.

Finally, she sighed. "Thank you, Zeke. I don't think I've ever seen anything that moved me as much in my life."

He squeezed her shoulders, knowing this was the moment he ought to let go, step away. He didn't. Instead, he stroked her slim arms gently. "My pleasure."

And it was. How often had he wished for someone with whom to share a moment like that? In spite of his father, he'd been close to his siblings and it was natural for him to wish for someone to see what he saw, to share those magical mornings with. He pointed toward the valley. "Did you see that?"

"Yes. It's even more beautiful than I expected. You're so lucky to have a place like this."

That was one way to look at it. "I am," he heard himself say. The weird emotion—that strange hope—grew another notch in his chest. It scared him.

"If you want to go back to bed, you can," he said, stepping away.

"No." She ambled to the edge of the porch, gazing out at the landscape. He found his attention snagging on her strong legs, bare under the shorts. Without warning, he remembered the sight of her smooth, graceful back last night, the tiny glimpse of white breast he'd seen under her arm. The memory both aroused and shamed him. "I'm sorry about last night, Miss Mary."

Impossible to read the look in her eyes just then. He was sorry if he'd said anything to break the spell of the magic, glorious morning. As awkward as a thirteen-year-old, he glanced away.

"I peeked, too," she said, and a tinge of rose colored her cheeks.

"No, you didn't. I kept my eyes on you."

"Not last night," she said and folded her arms. "The day at the river, back in Kismet."

He remembered the morning and grinned. "Guess we're even, then, huh?"

She nodded, smiling in return.

Just that fast, Zeke was slain. Early gold light washed over her, gilding the silky cap of hair, edging the curve of a small ear, cascading down her long white neck. Her tank top had slipped on one side, giving him a broad view of her shoulder. It would be so easy, he thought, so easy to flick those straps from her shoulders and send that ugly little shirt slipping away.

The vision hurt. The swelling wish for—what?—collapsed like a balloon in his heart, and he remembered the others. Not so many as some might expect, but enough women to know he couldn't get it right, that he'd take what Mattie offered so generously, then destroy it, somehow or another. This time, he'd just leave it alone.

"If you want to go on and get dressed," he said with effort, "we can have some breakfast. Maybe go hiking." That would keep them busy, at least.

"Will you show me how that shower works first? I'm dying to get cleaned up."

The shower. He stared at her for a long minute, willing himself to be an adult, to behave as if he'd learned how to control his more carnal impulses. Damn. The shower.

"Is that a problem?" she asked. "I can just wash up, instead."

"No. No, it's not a problem. Get your stuff and I'll show you how it works."

Barefoot, shirtless, Zeke led the way. Mattie followed, trying to keep her eyes to herself. It was hard. Each step he took made the muscles shift and ripple in his long, strong back, in his hips below the snug-fitting jeans, in his thighs.

The shower stunned her. She'd been expecting a little building, like the outhouse. This was just a small wooden platform, built about a foot off the ground with wide slats to let the water pass through to the ground beneath. A pipe led from inside the wooden building with the sauna to a shower head on the wall. "This is it?" she asked.

Zeke looked uncomfortable. "It works pretty well— I've got it rigged to draw water from the pool inside. It's not gonna be real hot, but it's warm enough." He showed her how to make the water run. "Short bursts work best. Get wet, then soap up and shower off."

Mattie nodded.

"I won't peek this time," he said. "Promise. I'll get breakfast going."

"Thanks."

He left her, disappearing around the building. He wouldn't be able to see her from the cabin, that much was sure, and it was very private land. No one but the deer and birds as audience.

Still, she hesitated, standing next to the platform in the warm morning sunlight, her towel and fresh clothes hugged close to her chest as if in protection. She looked around, gnawing the inside of her lip.

The vista of the valley was visible over the top of the trees from the shower, the same view as from the back porch of the cabin. She was sure Zeke had positioned it here deliberately, but all that scenery made her feel even more vulnerable.

Maybe she could just wash up a little, forget about the shower. Except she itched all over from yesterday's dust and sweat and rainwater.

Slowly, she put her things down and stood up, taking one more quick glance over her shoulder to see if there was anything or anyone around. There wasn't, of course. Just Mattie and the open vista.

She took a breath and shed her tank top, then her shorts. A ripple touched her skin and all the parts that had never seen real, live daylight felt extraordinarily exposed. She stepped onto the platform.

Standing there nude, with a soft breeze blowing over her, with that panorama before her, something happened. It wasn't shameful as she'd thought it might be. Nor was it arousing, though there was something empowering about shedding everything this way.

A burst of something holy and wild and real filled her, and with great reverence, she gazed around her, feeling no longer an observer of the landscape, but a part of it. Without knowing why, she lifted her arms and tipped back her head to the sunlight, letting wind and sun touch her breasts.

Had she ever been aware of her body like this? Had she ever known the comfort of her body, the wonder of having arms and legs and breasts and hips?

Thank you, she breathed, but didn't know to whom she breathed it, Zeke or God or the mountain. As if in

LAY
OUETTE'S

D YOU GET
REE BOOKS
. FREE GIFT
ND MUCH MORE

THE PAGE AND
YOURSELF IN

PLAY "LUCKY H
AND GET . . .

★ Exciting Silhouette Intimate I
★ "Key to Your Heart" Pendant

THEN CONTINUE
LUCKY STREAK V
SWEETHEART OF

1. Play Lucky Hearts as instructed o

2. Send back this card and you'll rece
   Intimate Moments® novels. These
   $3.50 each, but they are yours to k

3. There's no catch. You're under no
   anything. We charge nothing—Z
   shipment. And you don't have to
   number of purchases—not even

4. The fact is thousands of readers en
   mail from the Silhouette Reader Se
   convenience of home delivery...the
   novels months before they're availa
   our discount prices!

5. We hope that after receiving you
   remain a subscriber. But the cho
   or cancel, anytime at all! So why
   invitation, with no risk of any ki

SILHOUETTE'S

*With a coin –
scratch off
the silver card and
check below to see
what we have for you.*

245 CIS AQM3 (U-SIL-IM-08/94)

YES! I have scratched off the silver card. Please send me all the free books and gift for which I qualify. I understand that I am under no obligation to purchase any books, as explained on the back and on the opposite page.

NAME _____

ADDRESS _____ APT.

CITY _____ STATE _____ ZIP

| **Twenty-one gets you 4 free books, and a free crystal pendant necklace** | **Twenty gets you 4 free books** | **Nineteen gets you 3 free books** | **Eighteen gets you 2 free books** |

DETACH AND MAIL CARD TODAY

THE SILHOUETTE READER SERVICE™: HERE'S HOW IT WORKS

Accepting free books places you under no obligation to buy anything. You may keep the books and gift and return the shipping statement marked "cancel". If you do not cancel, about a month later we'll send you 6 additional novels, and bill you just $2.89 each plus 25¢ delivery and applicable sales tax, if any.* That's the complete price – and compared to cover prices of $3.50 each – quite a bargain! You may cancel at anytime, but if you choose to continue, every month we'll send you 6 more books, which you may either purchase at the discount price ... or return at our expense and cancel your subscription.

*Terms and prices subject to change without notice. Sales tax applicable in N.Y.

reply, a mountain bluebird flitted nearby, whistling, and Mattie laughed.

Following Zeke's instructions, she showered, and it was a delicious experience, as well. Going back up the hillside, dressed and clean, she found herself humming a song from the *Song of the South,* "Oh, What a Beautiful Morning."

Zeke crouched on the porch, putting something in two little bowls. One held water, the other sliced canned peaches. "What's that for?" Mattie asked, rubbing a towel over her hair.

"Rocky," he said, enigmatically. "You'll see. Come on inside. Breakfast is just about done."

A smell of baking greeted her as she stepped inside, leaving the door open behind her. Zeke bent and took a heavy cast-iron muffin tray out of the oven, and the scent of the oversize muffins made her mouth water. "Poppyseed muffins?" she said lightly. "I'm impressed."

"Well, don't be." He put the tray down on top of the stove and lifted his chin to an empty package of muffin mix. "Add water and pour."

She smiled as she helped herself to coffee, still humming with the powerful sense of well-being that had engulfed her at the shower. "They smell good."

"Go ahead. There's no butter, but you kind of get used to it without."

Mattie took a steaming muffin from the pan. Holding the coffee in one hand, the muffin in the other, she wandered the room, her gaze snagging on a trio of snapshots stuck with thumbtacks to the wall by the bookcase. She'd missed them earlier, for they were somewhat hidden by the shadows. Now she leaned forward to examine them, munching her breakfast.

The first was of a horse, beautiful even to Mattie's untrained eye—tall and lean with a glimmering black coat and a long tail. The next showed Zeke astride the horse, a worn cowboy hat on his head, smiling. She glanced over her shoulder, but he was studiously ignoring her to gaze out the door.

The third photo pinched her. Zeke with his arm thrown around the shoulders of a tall striking blond woman. A man knelt nearby, holding a trophy of some kind. The woman looked at Zeke with the kind of hungry, worshipful expression on her face Mattie knew she'd often given him. In the background were the noses of three horses hanging over a fence like the one just outside. "Was this picture taken here?" she asked, pointing to it.

"No." He didn't look around.

Mattie lifted an eyebrow at the abrupt answer. The bear had a thorn in his paw, but she'd be damned if she'd try to pull it out. Not right now. "Who is the woman?"

"Somebody I used to know." He still didn't look at her. His shoulders held a rigid tenseness that spoke volumes of fury.

She tried one more time. "What did you win?"

He stood up. "Nothing." The word was harsh, and he still didn't look at her as he poured a second cup of coffee. "Why don't you mind your own business?"

Mattie smiled to herself as she walked away from the picture. Yes, sir, a big thorn. Going over to the stove, she took another muffin and peeled away the paper, settling in the single chair as she looked around her again with new eyes.

Through the window, she saw the empty corral. Even she knew what a corral was. It held animals of some sort or another, and she would bet money this one had been built for horses. It had been a while, though, since there had been any in there, if there ever had.

She touched the stallions on the blanket and glanced at Zeke. His tattoo was covered, but it did have the same stallion on it.

She glanced at the books. Horses. On the wall hung a calender. Horses. She looked at his boots. Not the kind of drugstore cowboy kind of boots she'd seen so often in Kansas City, but the real thing, hardworking boots she'd guess he'd owned for a long time.

So what was a horse-crazy man doing on a motorcycle, flipping hamburgers in a nothing little bar in a nothing little town?

She didn't have a chance to answer the question in her mind. At that moment, he turned around with a secretive smile. "Rocky's here."

Chapter 9

Brian Murphy shed his coat with a furious gesture. "She can't just disappear like this!"

Vince, peeking out the curtains of their motel room in Albuquerque, said, "We'll find her, Bri. Just a matter of time."

"We don't have much time," Brian retorted, shoving his fingers through his red hair until it stood on end. "I've got work to do. If I don't get that bitch out of my way, the cops will get me first. Without her, there's no case."

"I don't know why you didn't let me and one of the other guys take care of her. You could be home right now, drinking bourbon."

Brian narrowed his eyes. "This is personal."

"Yeah, well, I wish you'd mellow out. You're making me nervous." Vince flicked the curtain in place and picked up the phone. "I'm going to order something from room service. You want anything?"

Brian shook his head no, then thought better of it. "Bottle of bourbon."

He paced as Vince placed the call, unable to quell the restless energy that was his trademark. In an effort to curb the rage threatening to engulf him, he breathed in slowly, then out, trying to find his center.

For a minute, it helped. Then he thought of Mattie again and the murderous fury returned. He'd outsmarted business partners, manipulated the law and the police and outmaneuvered some of the most powerful drug lords in the country—one naive woman would not be his undoing.

It did not improve his mood to acknowledge the mistake was largely his own. He'd made the unforgivable error of underestimating Mattie O'Neal, seeing only a sweet, alluring secretary with a headful of simple dreams. He'd accepted her intelligence as his due, a necessary component in a wife, but his focus had always been on the nurturing end of her personality. What he'd seen in Mattie was an uncomplicated woman who'd make him an undemanding wife, and take care of their children. He'd never intended for her to find out that his fortune was built on shipping black-market guns and pharmaceuticals to profitable and illegal markets.

Breathe in, breathe out. Who would have guessed Mattie could steal a car? Disappear for weeks on end? His stomach burned with a sick, furious churning as he thought of the wild-looking champion who'd whisked her away. She hadn't even given Brian a chance to explain—she'd shacked up with the first available man to come her way. It had taken him almost a year to get her into his bed. A lousy year.

"Bourbon's here," Vince said, paying the waiter.

Brian poured three fingers straight and tipped it back. The heat burned clear to his belly and performed its miracle of clearing his brain. "What'd you get on this Zeke Shephard?"

Vince, sitting down to a sandwich and a beer, tugged a notepad from his suit coat. "Ran a horse-breeding operation west of here till two years ago when the business went bust. Not much else on him."

"Partners? Family? Anything?"

Vince nodded. "Had a partner by the name of John Reese. He married some horse society type and took over Shephard's business."

Brian nodded, unbuttoning his shirt. "I'll shower and we'll go see him."

Rocky, it turned out, was a raccoon. He waddled onto the porch and paused cautiously, looking around, then eased up to the small bowls.

"Oh, look!" Mattie cried softly, clutching Zeke's arm reflexively. "They really do wash things."

"Yeah." He covered her hand on his arm as if to hold it there. The word was soft. "So danged cute."

The raccoon took a peach in his tiny black hands and dipped it in the bowl of water, swishing it around thoroughly, rubbing at the fruit until he seemed satisfied and sat back on his haunches to eat it. He made a little noise, a soft growl of satisfaction.

"Once," Zeke said softly, his deep voice resonant even at such a low level, "I put some spare biscuits out there and he washed them until they fell apart. Liked to broke my heart seeing him try to pick all those sloppy pieces out of the bowl."

He slipped to one side on the chair, and motioned for her to sit down on the arm. Mattie did. "Does he let you come out when he's eating?"

"Sometimes. Not usually when I've been gone, though. It's like he has to make sure all over again that I'm not gonna eat him."

Mattie smiled. The creature was unbelievably precious. The slim black mask over his eyes, the alert little ears. Like a cross between a sweet dog and a clever cat. "He looks smart."

"They are." Zeke watched Rocky with a bemused expression on the handsome features, and the expression made her heart flip. "A neighbor used to have one when I was a kid. Caught it in the forest and brought it home. We used to take it pieces of banana and stuff like that. He was really cute.

"But people all over started having trouble with chicken coops and vandalism. One old coot went out to his garage one morning and found a huge mess, oil cans on the floor, sand scattered all over the place, the curtains shredded." He chuckled. "For a while, the cops thought it was teenagers, but they found out it was that raccoon. He not only learned how to open his cage, but also how to keep his owner from knowing he could."

Mattie laughed softly, but the animal heard her and paused, looking up from the peach with an alert ear cocked toward her. For long moments, they stared at each other through the open door. Mattie found herself gripping Zeke's shoulder, felt his hand tighten over hers.

The raccoon dropped the peach he was eating, and Mattie thought with a pang that he was going to leave, that she'd chased him off. Instead, he plucked a new peach from the bowl and started scrubbing it clean.

Realizing how she gripped Zeke's shoulder, she forced herself to let go of him. "I'm glad I didn't chase him away."

He nodded. After a minute, he said gruffly, "The woman in the picture, her name is Amanda Shaw." He fell silent again, but Mattie waited without speaking, and he went on. "The guy is John Reese. He used to be my partner. They're married now."

Mattie watched his face carefully. His gaze was fixed on the raccoon, so she saw Zeke in profile. The sharp cheekbones with the hollows below, the firm, sensual mouth, the black fringe of long eyelashes above the troubled green eyes. His hair swept back from a forehead tense with remembered—what? Fury? Sorrow?

Regret. The small lines around his eyes looked taut, too, and she wanted to smooth the tightness away with her fingertips. Had he lost his love to his partner?

"And the horse?" she asked gently, lightly. "What was the horse's name?"

He turned, looking up at her, the color of his eyes so clear, the emotion so cloudy, it made her stomach hurt to look at him. His gaze scanned her face with a sharp intensity, as if he didn't know whether he could tell her. "Othello."

So close. The light coming through the door highlighted every detail on his beautiful face. She saw a hint of whiskers on his chin, a sharp jagged scar at the edge of his right eye, another through his lip.

Impulsively, she touched the scar on the edge of his eye. It was slightly hollow. It must have been a bad one, when it was fresh, and she wondered how old he had been. Six, eight, ten?

He didn't wince at her touch or look away, simply let her trace the old wound lightly with her finger, saying nothing. She wanted to know the history of this mark, and the one on his mouth, and the harsh puckered one on his back. She wanted to go back in time and be there for the child he'd been, bandage him and ease him, hold him so he could cry away the pain.

Something flickered in his eyes, something deep and long-buried, a wild flash Mattie responded to on some primal level. She opened her palm on his dark, hard face and traced the jutting edge of cheekbone, the smooth hollow beneath, the line of his jaw. Through it all, Zeke stared at her with a boiling emotion in his eyes she didn't try to name.

Sitting so close to him, she felt again his odd, powerful heat, and that scent of warming earth that came from his skin, from his body, an almost unbearably seductive smell.

She touched his dark eyebrows, each one, and smoothed her fingers over his forehead. At last, bravely, she touched his hair. Coarse, thick, and somehow still silky, as if he'd washed it in rainwater.

"I miss the feeling of hair all around me," she said at last, threading her fingers through the length of his on his shoulders. "The way it swishes and swirls on your skin and the way it feels when you brush it." Lost in some strange place, driven by an instinct she didn't question, she smoothed her fingers through his scalp, over and over.

"Mattie," he said, lifting a hand to her arm, as if to stop her.

But he didn't. His hand lit on her elbow and skimmed to her wrist, and Mattie smiled. The rigid lines in his face were easing under her touch, the tautness around his eyes relaxed. The lingering boil of emotion in his eyes hadn't changed, but Mattie knew with certainty that it could.

Never in her life had she been brave or bold. She'd always waited her turn, waited to be asked if she needed something, tried to keep out of people's way and not be a bother.

And time after time after time, she saw the best coat go to another girl; was passed over for a promotion that should have been hers; lost out on seconds at the dinner table.

At that moment, sitting on the arm of the chair, with Zeke's hair tumbling through her fingers and his eyes boiling with that dangerous lostness, Mattie leaned forward and claimed something. She kissed his cheek, gently, catching a tiny bristle of beard against her lip. His hand tightened on her wrist, almost convulsively, but he didn't shove her away, just held on. For one brief instant, she pressed her forehead to his temple. "I'm sorry you lost your horse," she said quietly, then forced herself to stand up normally, as if there had been nothing extraordinary at all in the moment they'd spent so closely unified.

For the space of a few breaths, Zeke didn't move and Mattie saw that he was struggling on some internal level. He stared at her intensely, then looked away, to the valley visible through the door.

Finally, he cleared his throat. "Why don't we take that hike? I'll show you around the land." His voice betrayed nothing.

"I'd love to."

"Don't suppose you have a swimsuit in that mess of rags, do you?"

"Rags?" she said, and laughed. "No, I don't. Is there a place to swim?"

"Yeah. I'm gonna swim in shorts. You can probably make do with that dowdy old tank top you wear to bed."

"Okay." Mattie took it from the pile.

He winced. "I've got half a mind to go to town and buy you some decent clothes, woman. I haven't seen such an ugly collection in one hell of a long time."

Unoffended, Mattie smiled. Aside from the jeans and T-shirt she'd purchased the first morning after she stole Brian's car, and the dress she'd worn to play pool in, his assessment was on the money. "I couldn't afford to be picky. I've never really cared all that much for clothes, anyway."

"Is that right." The phrase wasn't a question.

Mattie looked up. "People who live in glass houses shouldn't throw stones," she said.

"What's wrong with my clothes?"

"Nothing except you wear the same white shirts and jeans five days out of six." She gestured to the uniform he wore now. White cotton shirt, buttoned to the third button, sleeves rolled to just below the elbow, jeans, boots. "Tell me I'm wrong."

He turned his lips down and looked a the shirt. "They're comfortable and cheap and I can toss 'em out when they get messed up. That's just sensible."

"Oh," she said with a touch of irony. "Men are allowed to be sensible, but women have to be pretty. Got it now."

His smile was natural, teasing and utterly dazzling. "That's right."

Mattie rolled her eyes.

"You really aren't interested in clothes?" he asked, filling a backpack with things from the shelves.

"I'm really not," she replied. She sat on the edge of the bed to tie her desert boots.

He made a little grunt of surprise and put a can opener in the front pocket of the pack. "Not even some kind of fancy blouse or some go-to-town shoes?"

Mattie considered that. "Black velvet and pearls for the symphony, when I was a little girl. Red shoes like Dorothy in *The Wizard of Oz*, but only if they were really magic. A dress like Cinderella in the movie." She grinned. "Does that make you feel better?"

He inclined his head, his expression musing. "I think you haven't let yourself want anything."

Mattie shrugged. "What's that old prayer—help me to accept what I can't change?"

"I guess." He swung the pack over his broad, powerful shoulders. "Come on. Let's get moving before the morning is completely gone."

Zeke knew everything, Mattie thought later, walking happily behind him as he led the way downhill. He knew the names of trees and flowers and the tiny orange mushrooms growing in a grove of trees. He told her that if she ever got lost, she should look for lichen on the trunks of trees to keep her pointing north. He showed her the tracks of animals in the soft damp ground, and knew which ones belonged to which. It amazed and delighted her that he knew so much.

They'd been hiking for hours, following a trail barely visible unless one knew it was there, up the mountain, clear to the summit, which looked out on the surrounding land for hundreds of miles. Zeke pointed out trees and plants, outcroppings of various kinds of rocks, knew the name of each peak they could see.

Now, pleasantly grimy and winded from the long, long walk, she said, "I thought we were going to go swimming. I'm hot."

"Almost there," he said, ducking under a branch. He turned his feet sideways to gain purchase in the sandy soil, and Mattie followed suit, skittering and sliding a little. Warm, strong sunlight beat down on her head, and she knew her nose would be sunburned tonight.

"Here we go," Zeke said, rounding an enormous red-brown boulder. He gestured proudly. "The swimming hole."

Mattie couldn't help the sigh of wonder that escaped her lips. The clearing was cozy, guarded on three sides by glittering aspens that whispered a welcome. At their feet was a small green pool, fed by a spring that gurgled up from the ground, and the redolent, curious scent of the water filled the air with an almost aphrodisiac quality.

The pool and the trees, with the vast blue Colorado sky stretched above it, would have been breathtaking enough, but on the fourth side of the pool was a vista Mattie couldn't believe, a view of a high plain, far below, dusted with green and yellow and fields of orange flowers, and beyond that, mountains rising from the plain in furry blue. "Oh, Zeke," she said, and touched his arm. "This is incredible!"

"Not amazing?" He smiled at her, the expression unguarded and deeply pleased. "Why don't you go change?"

She didn't need to be urged twice. Eagerly, she dashed into the trees, stripped and slipped into her tank top and shorts. This time she left on her bra—the shirt was not exactly a good fit.

Zeke had plunged into the water ahead of her, and before she could join him, he surfaced, shaking hair from his eyes. Sunlight blazed over the slick expanse of his shoulders, blazed over his muscled chest and arms—and Mattie was so dazzled she forgot her own self-consciousness and allowed herself to stare.

"Come on in."

Mattie put her folded clothes in a pile on the ground and walked to the edge of the pool, pleasurably aware of the appreciative caress of his eyes on her body. At the edge, she paused to stick a toe in the water.

"It's like bathwater!" she exclaimed.

"Hot springs," he said. "It'll cure whatever ails you."

She met his gaze as he walked toward her, the water sluicing away from his body to show the flat, hard belly and lean hips, clad in jean shorts. "Is it deep?" she asked.

"Not really." He stopped with the water at his waist. "I dug it out, and I got tired of digging after a while. 'Bout shoulder height on you, I imagine."

Mattie walked in, amazed. "You dug it out?" she asked, shaking her head. "There's nothing you can't do, is there?"

"Well, it takes a pretty clever guy to dig a hole," he said, light glinting his eyes. He held out his hand to draw her into the water.

"I couldn't do it," she parried, and let his hand go as she reached the deeper part of the pool. "And I couldn't build a house or raise horses or—"

He touched her mouth, smiling. "Hush up, Miss Mary, and just enjoy yourself."

She smiled. "All right."

The pool was one of Zeke's favorite places on earth, and it never failed to fill him with a buoyant sense of full-heartedness. Today was no different.

No, he corrected, today was even better. Mattie had the rare ability to forget herself and play. She splashed and swam, ducked under the water to disappear in the soft green world to grab his ankles under the water.

Damned if he didn't find himself doing the same thing. Playing. Ducking and hiding and diving and splashing, like he was fourteen. Their laughter—his as much as hers—filled the still mountain noon with music.

And also like he was fourteen, Zeke found himself indulging the delectable, safe pleasure of touching her like this, grabbing her smooth long legs under the water, feeling her breasts nudge him as they water-wrestled. Like a boy, he spent the time lazily, pleasantly aroused.

Seeing her like this, animated and vibrantly enraptured by the mountain air, he couldn't imagine how he'd ever thought her ordinary-looking. The sun had coaxed warm color into her cheeks and her big brown eyes blazed with vibrant emotion—happiness now, mischief then, a simple flash of hunger, pure and direct. Her cap of hair clung to her well-shaped head and rivulets of water ran over the long pretty neck as if to invite him to taste the path of her throat.

And every time she left the pool for a minute—to dry her face, or get a sip of water from the canteen or rest for a minute in the thick, hot sunshine, he just about came undone.

She didn't wear tight clothes, so he'd never really seen how voluptuously curved she was. The wet cotton T-shirt and shorts clung to every tiny detail. Full breasts, a slim waist and a beautiful, plump rear end that liked to drive him right around the bend.

Now she swam easily toward the source of the pool, and leaning against a boulder at the other side, Zeke watched her through half-closed eyes. The shirt billowed around her, slipping off her shoulders to show the teeny strap of her bra and her gleaming skin.

The spring bubbled out of a fissure in granite, a little above the pool. Water sprayed over a shelf of rock to form a softly splashing waterfall. Mattie ducked under it, letting the spray tumble over her face.

Zeke's arousal, pleasantly low-key until that moment, took a sharp turn toward the urgent. Her expression was sybaritic, wholly focused on the pleasure of the moment, and her sexy, sexy mouth was slightly parted, slick with the spray. She braced herself by clinging to the rock behind her, and the position exposed her breasts in full glory—full and white and about to fall out of that ugly little top, which suddenly seemed about a thousand times sexier than any bathing suit he'd ever seen.

She probably had no idea how stretched that fabric had become, how little it covered. Her bra was a thin beige, made of plain cotton lace, with a tiny pink flower at the center. Through the wet fabric he saw the dark tips of her nipples.

Half-drugged with the need he'd denied for days now, he left his place at the opposite side of the pool and drifted toward her silently. When he reached her, she opened her eyes and he saw by her sharp intake of breath that he'd startled her.

Before she could move, he ducked his head under the waterfall and covered that luscious mouth with his own.

A small noise of surprise came from her throat, but she made no move to get away from him. The spill of warm spring water splashed down over their heads, making their lips slick, giving a musky flavor to their tangling tongues. Zeke pulled back infinitesimally to let the water trickle between them, tasting water and Mattie's mouth all at once. Her mouth opened and they drank together of the mineral-heavy water from deepest earth and traded the taste with each other, openmouthed. He slid his mouth along her jaw, licked her cheek, her ear, her neck—found again her mouth and suckled it the way he'd wanted to since he'd first laid eyes on her. Plump and sweet. He rubbed his tongue on that plumpness, aware of a wildness rising in him—an unbearable, ungovernable hunger that filled his belly and chest and throat.

Driven by that need, he pinned her against the soft earthen wall behind her and trapped her with his arms and legs. He felt the wildness in him with a tiny part of his mind, felt the slight fear in Mattie as he surrounded her with himself. He struggled to pull himself under control, but as if she sensed it, she wrapped her legs around his waist under the water and held him there. Her arms came around his shoulders, and her water-cooled breasts, so thinly covered, pressed into his chest.

Zeke heard his control snap with a cracking sound. Roughly, he dragged her shirt from her shoulders, devouring her mouth, feeling her heat against his aching erection. She gasped slightly and her legs tightened, and now her hands skimmed restlessly over his chest and back, hungry hands, to match her hungry mouth that plucked and bit at his.

Still drugged on wild desire, he struggled with the clasp of her bra, and when it wouldn't come free, he tore it at the center, where the fabric was thinnest. Mattie cried out, but he captured the sound with his mouth, touching her with a need unlike anything he'd ever felt. Her skin was slick and smooth, her breasts white and full, tipped with cinnamon. He bent his head and tasted her, suckling the tips until he felt her hips moving against him, jarring his passion to a roaring level.

She opened her eyes, wide and brown, filled with a sultriness he must have known could be there. With a strong movement, she put her body against his, locking arms and legs tight around him. She stared at him with a strangely stricken expression, and began to move a little, below, her sweetness against his aching arousal.

He kissed her violently, wanting to somehow inhale her into himself, unable to stop the fury of his reaction, the trembling rocking hunger for her—so vast and all-encompassing, he couldn't stand it.

Mattie, flowing all around him, met his savagery. He clasped her hips hard against him, found himself biting her neck, laving her breasts with his tongue. He felt such unblunted, furious desire he thought he might die of it.

Sweet Miss Mary grasped handfuls of his hair to drag his head up to her, so she could kiss him—and she was strong, so much stronger than he'd believed. He kissed her, feeling the slight pain of her grip in his hair, feeling her teeth and his, and the bruising sharp blaze of their desire.

He tasted blood on her lips—and the moment shattered. With a rippling sense of horror, he lifted his head, pushing her away urgently to look at her. That beautiful, plump lower lip was split and beading blood; her neck showed a blazing bruise from his mouth, and another showed on her full white breast.

Shaken, he let her go abruptly and swam for the bank, afraid he would be sick before he could get away.

Chapter 10

Mattie paced the small space inside the cabin as another late-afternoon rainstorm rolled in, darkening the sky, shooting dramatic slashes of lightning through the gray. The air was almost oppressively still.

A film clip of the scene at the pool this afternoon played over and over in her mind, not in a smooth, orderly way, but in jerky bits: that blistering wildness that came from Zeke all of a sudden, as if his armor had split and let a new man out, this one not reserved or controlled or in the least bit civilized; the sudden claim of his mouth—she touched the bruised lips gingerly as she remembered; the urgent strength of his body.

Remembering, she felt a rustling over her nerves, an alertness in the faintly overused parts of her body. She had a bruise on her neck from his mouth, scarlet and vivid, and one lower on her breast; she couldn't look at them without feeling a sharp, deep throb in her belly.

His intensity had frightened her. She had to admit that. His need, breaking free all at once, had seemed more than she could manage—he seemed to need to devour her. His hands had been so rough, his mouth so hungry.

And yet, it had been like everything else with Zeke—vivid, overwhelming Technicolor. He hadn't hurt her at all, not even when his fierce kiss had split her lip. To her deep embarrassment, she found she'd rather liked it wild and intense like that.

In her pacing, she paused at the window. Zeke had disappeared into the sauna when they came back down the mountain, his silence unbroken all the way back to the cabin.

She had no idea what had made him surface so abruptly, what had made him push her away. With a stunned and plummeting sense of frustration, she'd watched him splashing awkwardly in his haste. Mattie had called after him, to tell him she was all right, but he ignored her, stumbling on water-heavy legs as he made his way toward the trees.

And then she'd realized she was standing waist-deep in the pool, her shirt bunched around her waist. Pierced, she sank under the water hastily and tugged the wet fabric over herself.

Now she paced to the stove and back to the door, peering out to the grayness beyond, watching the lightning come closer and shiver over distant mountains. A flicker of uneasy guilt touched her. Was what they'd done wrong? Was it wrong to feel such powerful desire? Was that what was meant by lust?

Absently, she touched the place on her neck that held the stain of his mouth, thinking of the way it had felt to have his tongue on her skin there. A rippling hunger weakened her knees. Was this lust?

She had no idea.

Was it dangerous? Would he have hurt her?

No. The feeling was very strong. It might have been intense, wild, but he wouldn't have hurt her. If she had wanted him to stop, it might have taken a minute to penetrate that haze of desire, but she knew without a doubt that he would have listened to her.

Mattie's eyes were drawn to the picture of the blonde on the wall, the woman who stared with such naked longing at Zeke. He seemed oblivious to the emotion in her eyes, and Mattie felt a stirring of sympathy for the woman.

There were men who couldn't accept love, and Zeke, with his history, was a likely candidate for that sort of emotional stunting. He'd said as much.

And yet, she thought of his eyes earlier, when the raccoon had been on the back porch. Mattie had touched his scars and seen a boiling in those beautiful eyes. He wanted to be able to reach out, to break free, but he didn't know how. He couldn't reach out to her when she was being tender with him, so his emotions had exploded at the swimming hole.

The question was, then, had the blond woman in the picture seen what Mattie had seen? Had she tried to breach his walls, and failed? Did Mattie have anything she could give Zeke Shephard that a dozen other women didn't have?

Did she dare reach out?

As if her turmoil drew him, he emerged from the mysterious little building, the interior of which she had yet to see. His hair was still damp, curling on his shoulders, and he'd changed into his usual uniform—the jeans and white shirt—except his feet were bare. The sight of those high, bare arches sent a bright pulsing hunger through her. She crossed her arms over herself in warning. A little chagrined, she also found herself covering the mark of his mouth on her neck with a carefully draped hand, and wished for her hair to draw around herself.

So it wouldn't seem as if she'd been waiting for him, Mattie hurried over to the bed and flung herself down on the pillows, picking up a book she'd attempted to read earlier. Then she wondered if the bed was too suggestive and sat up, intending to race over to the couch, but he walked in.

Before, when he'd gone to the sauna, he'd returned in much better spirits, but there was no such lightening on his face now. He brought with him such a dark presence, it was almost frightening. He stared at her for a moment, and Mattie saw his gaze touch her mouth, the mark on her neck, saw the bleakness in his eyes. He seemed to hover at the door, staring at her, for an endless time. "We need to talk about some things, Mattie." His voice was heavy.

She nodded, waiting.

From his pocket, he took one of his rare cigarettes and lit it restlessly, blowing smoke toward the open door. A breeze snatched the smoke outside with a jerk. He lowered his head. "I'm sorry," he said, his voice almost a growl in the depths of his throat. The sound, Mattie thought, of a dangerously wounded animal.

"There's nothing to be sorry for," she said. Softly.

It seemed hard for him to meet her eyes, but he did it, finally. Mattie flinched inwardly at the blaze in his eyes. So haunted. "Right," he said.

She thought of the way he'd gentled under her hand earlier and stood up, intending to go sit beside him. "Zeke."

"Don't touch me, Mattie." The husky strain in his voice froze her.

She sank down on the bed.

"I'm gonna tell you a story," he said. "About the meanest son of a bitch that ever lived on this planet." He licked his lips, drew on the cigarette, stood up to put his back to her. "He wasn't but sixteen when he knocked up a local girl and had to marry her because that's how things were done then. He probably hated her before the baby was ever born, but her father promised he'd kill him if he disgraced her, so he stayed."

A small mournful cry sounded in Mattie's heart and she clenched her fists. She thought of her foster brother Jamie, and pressed her lips together.

The tone of Zeke's voice flattened, but the Mississippi drawl thickened as he spoke, and she knew how he'd spoken as a child. The words came slowly, one agonized sentence at a time. "By day, the man was a carpenter, so he was strong. By night, he was a drunk and practiced being strong with everybody around him—the woman that he hated, and raped so often she got a dull look in her eyes and couldn't hear anything around her, the dog." The voice lost all emotion. "But he really liked to beat up his kids. They didn't hit him back. Not at first."

He took a long draw on the cigarette and Mattie saw the trembling in his hands. His back was so rigid, she thought he might break. "The man had a son first, the rest were girls. Six of 'em. The boy didn't have too much trouble at first, not till the old man started on those girls."

Mattie closed her eyes and dug her fingernails into her palm to force herself to stay where she was.

"I think the first time I fought him, I was six or seven. He used to hit my mom a lot, and I was afraid of him, but he didn't pay me much attention. Liked to brag about me because I was big, strong—you know." He moved his mouth, as if he tasted something bitter. "He went after my sister that night and I just couldn't stand it."

Unconsciously, Mattie was sure, he touched the hollowed scar on his eye. Or maybe not unconsciously. Maybe he still remembered it. "You can guess who won."

For the first time since he'd started talking, he met her eyes. She nodded.

He shifted, stood up and went to the door to throw away the butt of his cigarette in an old coffee can he kept there. "It was pretty much war from that day forward. Sometimes he'd get to them when I was gone, and he had a lot of tricks to outsmart me and punish me—" His voice roughened so much, she had to lean forward to hear. "But I got him back sometimes, too. And most of my sisters made it out okay."

Mattie heard that "most" and the howling in her chest started anew.

He rubbed viciously at his face and made a low, pained noise. "I told you before that I don't ever intend to have a home and a family, and that's why. I've felt that violence in me, Mattie." His voice grew thick with self-loathing. "I felt it today."

Mattie jumped up and nearly flew across the room. It was the most purely impulsive gesture of her life, but she ran across the boards, and flung herself around his rigid form, her heart screaming.

"Stop, Zeke," she cried. "You didn't hurt me. That wasn't meanness." She clutched him, putting her face against his chest, smelling the scent of the water, and the scent of his skin and realized they were one and the same. She found herself close to tears as she held him, feeling the brittleness of his vulnerability like a precious jewel. "I wish there had been someone there to fight for you."

He unbent all at once, and she found herself swept up close, held gently and fiercely all at once.

Against her neck she felt the moist heat of his breath. "I don't know what happened this afternoon," he said. "I've never—it was so..."

"Don't think about it." She simply held him for long moments, until some of the rigidness left his body, until he took a breath. Terror. That's what she felt from him. Horror. That he might be his father, that there was the same evil lurking inside of him.

The pain in her heart trebled, and Mattie realized with a sinking feeling that she was very, very close to falling in love with him. The dawning knowledge made her ease away, lead him to a chair. "Sit down," she said. "Let me get you some coffee."

She didn't wait to see if he listened, but moved to the stove for the coffeepot and poured him a cup. His footsteps were nearly silent in bare feet, but she heard the chair creak a little under his weight. Mattie gave him coffee black and strong the way he liked it, and settled herself on the bed opposite.

"I had a foster brother once, named Jamie," Mattie said. "He's the one who taught me to play pool. He wanted me to be self-sufficient." She smiled briefly, but it was a painful memory, not often told. "I lived with his family for three years, from the time I was thirteen until I was sixteen. Jamie—" she paused, her throat growing thick "—was the only person I ever really connected with in any of those foster homes. He felt like my real brother."

"You don't have to tell me, Mattie."

"Yes, I think do." She stared at him, and she knew he understood what was coming. "Jamie's father beat him to death when I was sixteen, and Jamie was eighteen." She couldn't stop the tears that welled up in her eyes, but willed her voice to stay calm. "At least you got out," she said on whisper.

"What a pair we are," Zeke said, shaking his head. The smallest hint of a smile touched his lips. "Couple of hard-luck stories, huh?"

Mattie smiled ruefully. "Maybe we should run away and join the circus."

The half smile became whole. "I ran away and joined the rodeo."

"I ran to the ivory towers of the university life. It seemed so safe."

A silence fell between them, filled with the things each had learned about safety and dreams. For once again, they shared something—the safe enclaves had betrayed each of them.

And now Mattie had invaded what she knew was Zeke's sanctuary. "I think you should take me back to Pagosa Springs and let me catch a bus to Denver. I'm obviously causing problems—and I hate to repay your kindness like that."

"It isn't you, Mattie. It's me."

"Whoever it is, I think it's plain this won't work. I'm grateful for your help, but it would be best for me to just move on now."

"Mattie, you can't keep running. He'll find you and kill you." He jumped up, topped his coffee, turned around. "Why don't you turn yourself in? I'll even go with you if you want me to, stay with you until you get things together."

"No." Mattie said the word more loudly that she intended, and made a conscious effort to calm her voice. "You don't know him, Zeke. You just don't know." A blinding flash of the blood on the floor of the warehouse gave her a nauseated feeling. "You just don't know."

"All the police want is some help."

"If I go back to Kansas City, Brian will kill me."

"There's a warrant out for his arrest. He can't go to Kansas City."

"He doesn't have to! All he has to do is pick up the phone."

Zeke took a breath, hands on his hips. "I think you're overestimating his power."

"Maybe I am." She shrugged. "Better safe than sorry."

"The police can take care of you, Mattie. They have experience—witness program, protective custody, all kinds of things."

Mattie gripped the cup between her hands so hard she thought it might break. "No," she repeated. "Just take me to the nearest bus station and I'll get out of your life."

"Have you given any thought to what this means, woman? Are you going to run the rest of your life, dashing from one little town to the next?"

"He'll get tired of looking eventually," she said with more certainty that she felt. "If Katherine Anne Porter could hide for all those years with FBI posters hanging in every post office in America, a little nobody like me can do it forever."

"That's no kind of life, Mattie. Don't give him that much power over you. How can you find somebody to fall in love with and give you that family you want if you can't ever tell anyone the truth about who you are?"

"It's none of your business what I plan to do, Zeke! It isn't your problem. It's mine and I'll take care of it, okay? Just take me down to Pagosa Springs and I'll catch a bus from there."

"I can't do that, Mattie," he said, carefully putting his cup down on the stove. "I won't."

"I'll walk back down there if I have to."

"No, you won't."

She glared at him. He was right. With a sigh, she flung herself backward on the bed. "Fine. I'll just stay here and drive you crazy."

"Won't matter," he said without humor. "I'm already nuts."

She glanced up, but he was lighting a lantern. Off to the barns, no doubt, or someplace else. To her surprise, he held it out. "Take this on down to the sauna and sit in there a little while. It'll clear your head."

"Like it cleared yours?"

He lifted an eyebrow. "Sometimes nothing will do it, but I think it'll make you feel better."

Mattie took the lantern.

Much to her surprise, he was right. The sauna was far less primitive than she'd expected; in one corner stood a concrete incinerator where a fire burned. A two-by-two pool of warm mineral water—no doubt fed by the streams all around—sat in the middle of a wooden floor. Two benches, one high, one low, and wide enough for a person to lie upon comfortably, were nailed to one wall. Mattie stoked the fire and splashed water on the exterior of the incinerator as Zeke had instructed, and the experience was even more sybaritic than the shower.

Sitting in the comfortable dimness, her feet dangling in the small pool, her back braced against a bench, Mattie sighed. She was secretly relieved that he'd not agreed to her request to be taken to Pagosa Springs. Everything about this place was designed to please the senses—which said a lot, she decided, about the sensual nature of the prickly, beautiful Zeke himself.

Her debt to him was growing like a wild vine. He'd saved her life, opened her eyes to possibilities she could never have dreamed existed and had awakened something deeply passionate within her. Even now, there was a lingering, achy restlessness in her body, a longing only Zeke could quench.

But he wouldn't. He was honorable. He thought he would hurt her.

Lazily, she splashed water on the incinerator, over and over until thick steam filled the small room. It rippled down in gray clouds, caressing her face, her body, with ghostly fingers. Her skin glowed with it, and her blood had slowed to a languorous steady thrumming.

What would he do if she seduced him?

The thought came from nowhere, and yet it must have been hovering nearby, for it was fully formed and solid. What would he do?

She moved her feet in the water, vaguely enjoying the sweep of water over her toes. He'd probably been seduced once or twice, and likely by women far more experienced that she in such matters. Would Mattie make a fool of herself? What if he resisted or didn't want to make love to her?

Well, she amended, she was pretty sure he *wanted* to—but that didn't mean he wouldn't resist. In fact, he probably would. If she tried it. If.

But wasn't that lust? Where did lust end and something deeper begin? From the first moment she'd laid eyes on him, Mattie had wanted his body.

It shamed her. Zeke deserved better than the lascivious thoughts of tittering waitresses. He deserved better than a woman plotting to get him to make love to her against his better judgment. He had a right to the same respect a woman would ask of a man.

He'd been kind enough to bring her to his private sanctuary, give her shelter and feed her and entertain her, and she'd repay it by asking for the one thing he wanted to keep.

No. She wouldn't. She'd dress demurely and stay away from mountain pools with him and make sure she did nothing at all to tempt him. And as soon as he'd let her, she'd get out of his life entirely.

The prospect gave her very little pleasure.

Brian pulled out a map of Colorado. "Pagosa Springs," he said, trailing his finger over the thin red lines. "Here it is. About four hundred miles. Maybe we can get there by tomorrow night."

"Whatever you say, boss." Vince swilled a beer. "Whatever you say."

Chapter 11

Zeke had made a fire in the fireplace when Mattie returned, and the flames combined with the dancing light of the lanterns to create a cheery feeling in the room. He smiled at her when she came in. "How'd you like it?"

"You'd have to be dead to avoid appreciating that sauna."

"Yep, pretty much." He gestured toward the stove. "I made some supper. Nothing fancy, just some soup and biscuits, but I reckon it'll fill the hole in our bellies." He lifted the lid on the pot and stirred the contents, releasing a fragrant aroma into the air. "We should make a run to town tomorrow—get some supplies."

Mattie, relaxed to the point of bonelessness, simply nodded her agreement.

They ate for a while in companionable silence. Zeke seemed to have found some measure of calm in her

absence, because he treated her with his usual court-
liness, though he was very careful not to touch her.
Mattie found herself staring at the pictures on the wall,
and wanted to ask again what the trophy was for, but
didn't dare bring up anything that might rock the
fragile peace in the room.

Zeke, however, seemed to notice her gaze. "I built
this place from the money I earned, with those people," he volunteered, putting his bowl aside to stretch
out his legs.

"What happened?" Mattie asked cautiously.

His grimace was wry, but it covered a lot of pain.
"Woman trouble," he said and shook his head.
"Amanda happened. I should have known better."

There was about him an almost amused attitude,
and Mattie dared a question. "What should you have
known?"

He lifted his eyebrows ruefully. "That women bred
to that ritzy life don't ever let you get away unpun-
ished. She made up her mind the first minute we met
that she was gonna have old Zeke, and I don't think
she ever considered any man might not want her."

Mattie looked at the picture. The woman was
beautiful and trim, with the understated elegance of
money in every detail. "You didn't want her?"

He shrugged. "She was a good-looking woman and
all, but there was no real magic. Those were my wild
days with women, anyway—and my partner had the
hots for Amanda."

Putting her own bowl aside, Mattie stretched out
sideways on the bed, settling her head on her hand.
"What kind of business did you have?"

"I bred horses. Appaloosas. John, my partner, and
I met in Albuquerque at the rodeo, and over the years

we developed the business. Just a few horses at first, but by the end we had quite a herd, and a lot of business. Damn near got rich—by my standards, anyway.''

"And woman trouble brought you down."

"That's about the size of it. Amanda's daddy has racehorses—big-time money, too. He wasn't real crazy about her hangin' out with a two-bit operation like ours, but she honestly loved those horses, and she knew we needed her knowledge and her cash. She underwrote some of the stallions we bought, and a really fine mare.'' He looked at her meaningfully. "She gave me Othello as a present.''

Mattie glanced at the photo and wickedly guessed, "As long as you gave her your body in return."

Zeke laughed. "More or less. It wasn't giving her my body that was the problem, though. We had worked that out at the start—I told her I wasn't ever gonna settle down and raise babies, but she refused to believe me. When it finally sank in, she was fit to be tied.''

Hearing the reiteration of his intention to stay footloose, Mattie smoothed a hand over the stallions printed on the blanket. Wasn't there just a little bit of that belief in Mattie, too? That the right woman would settle this man, make him happy and see him father children? Chagrined, she bit the inside of her cheek. The right woman. Whatever woman happened to be madly in love with him. All of them probably had the same thoughts.

"Anyway," Zeke went on, his mood still remarkably light, "she plotted herself a real nasty revenge. John always wanted her in the worst way, and she used that—and all her daddy's money and connections in the horse world—to bring me down. I lost everything but this little cabin, but I had to sell Othello and the two other stallions that were mine free and clear to keep it.''

''When did all this happen?''

''Two years ago,'' he said. ''I've been drifting around the Southwest ever since.'' He lifted his cup in her direction. ''You woke me up, Mattie. I'd been feeling real sorry for myself for a long damn time, and you yanked me right out of it.''

She smiled, extraordinarily pleased that she'd been able to do something for him. ''I'm glad.'' She admired him lazily, without feeling the painful arousal from earlier. He looked exactly right in the pine-walled room, with firelight playing over his sharp, strong face, long legs crossed at the ankle. ''What are you going to do about it?''

He frowned. ''Good question. It's kind of a quandary. To get the cash I need for horses, I'd have to sell the land. Without the land, I have no place for the horses.'' He made a snorting noise. ''It took me ten years to save the cash I needed the first time around. Good stallions are expensive.''

''Can't you get a loan on the land?''

''Not without means to pay it back.'' He shrugged. ''I'll probably hire on with a ranch somewhere, just spend my winters here.''

Mattie flashed on the sauna and hot springs under cover of snow. ''I'll bet it's nice up here in the wintertime.''

''It is,'' he said quietly. ''Especially when it snows. Not everybody likes winters like that, but they make me feel like a million bucks.''

She smiled. "It's nice you got your dream, Zeke. That you got to grow up and have horses."

"What's your dream, Mattie?" he said, suddenly intense. "What did you want when you were a little kid in one of those foster homes?"

"All I really ever wanted was a family of my own," she said. "The past few years, I took up poetry because I liked the safety of that environment—universities are very protected places. And it seems not very fashionable to want to have babies and make a home, so I felt like I should come up with something else."

"Babies, huh?" Zeke said, and there was a strange tight sound to his voice. His gaze was focused on the fire. "I like babies a lot."

Mattie couldn't resist. "Is that an invitation?"

He glanced up, and Mattie saw the conflict in him. "You know, Miss Mary, if I were another kind of man, there'd be nothing I'd like better than to give you those babies."

His words, spoken in that low drawl, pierced her so deeply her breath fled. *Oh, yes.*

"Trouble is," he said, head cocked to one side, "I'd find some way to blow it all up before we were through, and you sure deserve better than that."

Mattie nodded. "Yes, I do."

He stood up by the fire a minute, seemingly undecided about something. Then he crossed the room and stopped by the bed, taking her hand to tug her upright. Mattie stared at him, bewildered by the swings of his moods.

He touched her cheek. "I like you better than any woman I've ever met," he said. He bent and pressed a warm kiss to her forehead. "Go on and get some sleep. We'll go into town tomorrow morning."

"Where are you going?" Mattie asked as he grabbed the sleeping bag from the floor.

"Just out to the porch, Miss Mary." His grin was wicked. "I think it'll be easier for me, if you don't mind."

"Won't you be cold?"

"I'll be fine."

And fine he was. In the cool mountain air, Zeke slept like a child, and awakened just as dawn tiptoed into the valley. Dew misted the pine trees around the porch and jeweled the grasses growing in stubby clumps all around the steps. A sprightly bevy of sparrows bounced in the yard, digging in the damp earth and chattering among themselves.

He listened. No cars. No planes. No electric wires humming. Only birds and the soft whisper of a morning breeze moving through the flat coins of aspen leaves. The silence gave him a powerful sense of well-being.

Something had shifted within him yesterday afternoon. So many painful emotions had torn at him, he thought he'd go insane with them. The old voices of derision and fury sounded like jackals in his brain.

While they'd been at their loudest, Mattie had flown across that cabin, surrounded him with herself, ignoring the fear he'd seen in her face, to hug him. Soothe him. In all his life, no one had ever done that. As a child, there'd been no one to do it; as an adult, he'd never let anyone close enough.

He'd never dreamed how good it would feel. How much sorrow and pain could drain so abruptly from him, like poisons spilling from a broken bottle. Maybe it was just the simple comfort of knowing there was someone who understood, who'd been there. The kind of childhood he'd known made most folks want to hide their heads.

His mind this morning was not so much on his childhood, as on the business he'd lost to Amanda and John. Losing it, the only thing he had, had nearly killed him. It had made him bitter and cynical.

This morning, what he wanted was to have his horses again. He missed the business and the money—that money had been mighty nice, and he was damned good at what he did—but he missed those horses with an almost physical pain.

Mattie had teased him about the books on his shelf, but she had him rightly pegged. He'd been horse crazy from the first time he'd laid eyes on one at the age of seven at a county fair. It had been a Tennessee walker, black and proud. Looking at it, with one arm in a cast from the second of his furious battles with his father, Zeke had believed in something beyond himself for the first time in his life. Tentatively, he'd reached up to touch that velvety nose. The horse had allowed it, and gazing into the big brown eyes, it seemed as if the horse understood.

What Zeke had learned was that he had a way with horses. When fairs and rodeos came to town, Zeke skipped school to spend his days and nights at the stables, hanging out until someone took pity on him and let him feed the creatures or clean the stables or whatever else needed doing. Didn't matter. He'd have gladly shoveled manure with his hands to get close to the horses.

And over the years, it became plain he knew the heart of horses. He knew when things weren't right with them—when they were in pain or feeling restless or whatever—more, he seemed to know what to do for them, without even thinking much about it.

It was a gift, the old stable hands maintained. Said he was half horse himself.

Yesterday, when he'd accused Mattie of allowing Brian to chase her into the shadows, when he'd asked her if she'd let Brian force her to give up her dreams, he'd been shocked to realize that was just what he'd done. Like a dog kicked once too often, he'd tucked his tail between his legs and come up here to hide, too weary to even want anything anymore.

He wondered if Mattie had ever seen a real horse. The thought made him smile. She'd loved absolutely everything about the country life he'd shown her—not once had she complained about the lack of electricity or plumbing facilities. She was blooming up here. He bet she'd like horses one hell of a lot.

Riding behind Zeke on his motorcycle in the clear of a summer mountain morning counted as equal parts pure pleasure and deepest torture. Mattie had no idea where they were going, only that he smiled over it, and that they needed some supplies. If they were going to get supplies, Mattie thought, he wasn't going to get rid of her just yet, and that was good.

In a way.

The bike sailed over the narrow highway like some liquid beast from a fantasy story, so fleet and easy she felt as if she were flying. Zeke's shirt billowed in the wind, against her fingers, and she could feel the freedom in him, in the easy play of muscles beneath her hands.

He was different this morning. Lighter somehow. The boiling was not entirely gone from his eyes—she doubted it ever would be—but there was mischief and light, too.

They stopped the first time in a little town, bigger than most along the little highway, with a proper square boasting drugstores, a grocery, filling stations at either end and several churches. "I need to see about getting some propane delivered," he said, pointing to a storefront office on the corner. "Why don't you go look around in the grocery store and pick out some food."

"I don't really know what to pick," she said, suddenly shy.

"Sure you do." He pressed several twenties into her hand. "Cans, mainly. Get some stuff with meat in it— I've got a propane cooler, but it's not hooked up at the moment, so we can't have any fresh meat. I'd like to have some fruit, too. Maybe some jerky."

"I have money," she said, and pressed his bills back into his hand. "Let me buy the groceries."

He gave her a half smile. "All right." He tucked the money into his shirt pocket. "It won't take me long. I'll meet you inside."

"How will we carry things back?"

He winked. "Trust me, Miss Mary. This ain't my first rodeo."

She laughed and went into the store, thinking it an intimate and pleasant act to be shopping for both of them, for the food they would consume. It was also deeply satisfying to be doing something as normal as shopping for groceries after such a long time. In Kismet, she'd had little storage space and only bought food a day a time, wary of spending more than she needed to spend for fear she'd have to leave at a moment's notice. Which she had.

Now she chose food for meals carefully. Good meals, balanced and varied, even if most of it had to come from cans. Idly, putting cans of chili and macaroni and cheese into the cart, she wondered what it would be like to live in a place like this all the time. Curious, she looked at the people in the store, wondering how their lives were different from the one she'd known. They were a tough-looking lot, with leathery skin and sturdy clothes. Even the young girls, in their shorts and tube tops and carefully applied makeup, looked strong, as if they could—

With a smile, Mattie realized she didn't even know what made them so strong. Taking care of animals? Weathering the elements? Braving such a rugged environment?

She didn't know, but she liked the strength she sensed. It felt important.

Zeke found her when she was dithering over the fruit. The oranges might last better, but they were more expensive than the apples. He smelled an apple. "Go for the oranges. These are last year's crop— they'll be mealy as hell."

She grinned. It was just the sort of thing he was always saying, as if everyone knew the names of mushrooms that grew in circles, or that foxes made a particular track or that apples had a certain undernote when they were old. "I've never met anyone who is as smart as you are," she said, lifting the apple to her nose.

"Smart?" He picked out a few of the apples and put them in a bag. "That's one thing I haven't been accused of on a regular basis."

"Well, you are." She grabbed the five-pound bag of oranges and gestured at the rest of the goods in the basket. "I tried not to get too much to carry, but I might have overlooked something."

He picked through the basket, lifting one or another of the items in his long-fingered hands, and Mattie liked the sureness of his movements. Cooking or shopping, chopping wood or riding a motorcycle, he was always utterly at home. It would be so strange to feel that confidence, she thought.

"Let's get the bigger size on the chili. I can eat two by myself. Other than that, you did just fine."

They loaded the groceries into a big leather pouch Zeke took from the compartment below the bike's seat and attached to the sissy bar on the back. "I'd like to stop at a friend's place on the way back, if you don't mind," Zeke said. "It's a little out of the way, but I think we have time."

A friend. It was the first time he'd mentioned such a creature. "I think I can fit it into my schedule."

His eyes twinkled, and without warning, he bent and brushed a quick kiss over her mouth, in full view of anyone walking by. "Come on, then."

Mattie climbed on, bracing herself for more delicious torture. This time, she sat a little closer, unable to resist his extraordinary heat, or the smell of his skin. She snuggled against his back, wrapping her arms around his stomach. Her thighs straddled his lean hips, and his hair touched her face.

Wicked thoughts pressed into her mind. It would be so easy to touch his thigh, to press her palm to that hard, jean-clad leg; so easy to explore his stomach and chest as he drove. It would be simple to unbutton his shirt, just enough to slip her hand inside, and feel that sleek, beautiful chest, touch his nipples and—

Her breasts felt heavy and needful and there was an ache low and deep, an ache that grew as she imagined even more wicked things she might do with her hands—if only she was brave enough. Some of them, she conceded, might cause a wreck.

She forced herself to sit upright again, tried to imagine the dance chaperon's hands between their bodies.

Zeke let go of the handlebars with one hand for a moment and touched her leg. He rubbed her thigh, just above the knee, as if he understood, as if he was not unmoved. Then he took her hand from his side and tugged her close again.

Mattie settled against him and went back to her wicked thoughts. Somehow, she didn't think they were in vain. Not anymore.

Chapter 12

The ranch was situated on a parcel of land in the high, flat valley floor. As they pulled into the driveway in front of a simple farmhouse, surrounded by outbuildings of various sorts, Mattie realized this was part of the land she could see from the hot-spring pool on Zeke's land. In the waste areas between the square, sturdy house and the barns grew wide clumps of the orange flowers that provided the splashes of color patchworking the valley.

She slid off the bike, hanging on to Zeke's shoulder for balance. He caught her around the waist, his green eyes alight with a clean, wild desire. "I want you, Mattie. We won't stay here long."

"I thought you said—"

He cut her off. "That was before."

She smiled, and dared to touch his neck, slipping her hand below his collar. "Before what?"

"Before I knew what I was getting into," he said, his voice low and seductive, his hand making circles on her tummy. One wide brush came very close to the lower swell of her breast and her response was instantaneous—her nipple lifted, as if to touch him. He lifted his gaze. "Do you want me, Miss Mary?"

She simply looked at him.

His fingers moved on her sides, skimmed upward in a subtle way. No one watching would have seen what he was doing. "Why don't you kiss me," he said, lifting his head. Waited.

Mattie swayed forward, holding her helmet in her hands, and pressed her lips to that irresistible mouth. He opened to her instantly and Mattie let herself drift for one tiny moment, let her herself explore again that unknown territory. She ended the kiss and straightened.

Zeke smiled. "One more time like that and I wouldn't give a rat's ass about anybody watching."

She winced and slapped his arm. "Your language!"

He sobered. "Just remember, Miss Mary, there are no roses and lace at the end of this path."

"I read you loud and clear, Captain," Mattie replied and slipped from his grasp to look around. Why did he always go out of his way to ruin the best moments?

The corrals here were not empty. Spotted gray and white horses, strong and muscular-looking, stood around a metal watering trough. "What kind are they?" Mattie asked.

"Appaloosas," Zeke said behind her. "The best workhorses around."

A man emerged from the barn, leading a graceful, high-stepping animal, all black, with a tossing head. The man spied Zeke and Mattie and grinned. "Finally broke down?" he called.

"I reckon," Zeke returned, but he was already moving forward. Mattie followed.

The man was in his late thirties, with coarse black hair and a powerfully angled face. The horse with him made a sudden noise, a high whining sound, and its graceful head tossed, jerked. The man let the reins go, and the horse galloped to the fence where Zeke stood waiting.

Mattie glanced at him. He'd climbed onto the fence and leaned over the top, softly whistling a series of notes. On his face was an expression Mattie had never seen—equal parts joy and sorrow. The horse hurtled forward, still making that strange sound. It reached Zeke and reared with a wild noise, then dropped and came forward, snuffling close to Zeke's neck, his hair, his face.

Zeke laughed, touching the horse on the neck, the nose, the chest. "Yeah," he said quietly, "I missed you, too, you old lug."

Othello.

Mattie glanced at the man in the corral. He caught her eye and grinned. "Enough to break your heart, ain't it?"

Mattie nodded, her throat tight. No one should have to be parted from an animal they loved as much as Zeke loved this one. No one. Even if, she thought darkly, that man could be a jerk at times.

"He's been restless all morning," said the man. "Must have sensed you were on your way."

"Maybe," Zeke said. "I've been thinking about him all week." He gestured toward Mattie, his scooping arm meant to urge her forward. "Mattie, this is my friend George Romero. George, this is Mattie O'Neal."

Mattie glanced at Zeke, surprised he'd given her real name. If he trusted the man, so did she. "Hi, George," she said.

George nodded. There was speculation in his dark eyes. "Are you visiting?"

"Um, more or less," Mattie replied. "Is it so obvious I don't belong here?"

He chuckled. "Most natives aren't too dazzled by a horse."

She smiled.

Zeke turned. "Reach into the pack and get a couple of apples, Miss Mary. Bring them here."

"Please?"

A flash of something crossed his eyes, too fast to be read. "Please."

She did as he asked. He took one from her. "Let me introduce you to Othello. He's not as bad-tempered as old George would have you believe, are you Othello?—just temperamental. But he'd stand on his head for an apple."

Making his hand a shelf, he put the apple in his palm and held it out. Othello almost delicately accepted the offering, and Mattie laughed. "He looks like he's at a society ball," she said.

"Try it," Zeke urged, pulling her closer. "He won't hurt you as long as you keep your hand flat and open. He doesn't know the difference between fingers and food."

"He might bite me?"

"Not if you keep your hand flat."

The horse looked at her with a big dark eye. There were eyelashes over the liquid irises, which startled her. The feathery black fringe gave the horse a curiously human aspect that gave her courage. Following Zeke's lead, she made her hand flat, put the apple in her palm and held it out.

She felt caught in suspended animation as Othello's great head descended. So close, she saw there were tiny threads of white in the hairs on his nose, and the big nostrils quivered. Once again, he opened his mouth and delicately plucked the apple from her palm with his teeth. Mattie had an impression of a soft whisk as the nose brushed her skin, then the apple was gone.

"Will he let me touch his nose, like you did?" Mattie asked.

"If he thinks you have another apple, he'll let you do anything you want." Zeke grabbed her by the waist and swung her onto the fence. "Go ahead."

Mattie clung with one hand and reached out with the other. The horse didn't shy away when her hand came close, and she gingerly touched that broad, strong nose. "Oh," she said softly. "It's so soft."

Zeke chuckled, and the sound was rich and warm. He slapped her bottom playfully. "I've got some business to take care of with George. You visit with Othello all you want to."

George pointed to the others, separated by a fence from the big black stallion. "Those are the *good* horses, over there," he said.

Mattie smiled. "Thanks."

The two men wandered off, talking quietly, and Mattie hung on the fence, stroking Othello's nose, absorbing the details of his body. In the early-afternoon sunshine, his coat gleamed with a shiny gloss, but it wasn't the coat of a dog or cat. Tentatively, she touched his shoulder blade. Warm skin with sleek hair over it. She traced the slim line of a vein and touched the jutting bone of his shoulder.

Othello hung by the fence, and it seemed to Mattie that he was watching Zeke. "You miss him, huh?" she said, brushing her fingers through the coarse black mane. It made her think of the pictures of horses in old Ireland, their manes braided and dressed with ribbons. "He misses you, too."

Othello whickered as if in answer. Mattie glanced over her shoulder to where Zeke stood with George. He wore his usual white shirt and jeans, and Mattie thought it to his credit he could make such ordinary clothes look so good. The jeans clung lightly to the long, hard stretch of his thighs, wrinkling at the knee. His rear end was just about perfect, Mattie thought, admiring it. He stood with one hand on his waist, his head down to listen to George, who was much shorter. His hair gleamed in the sun, dark-streaked with sun-coaxed blond.

As if he felt her gaze, he glanced over, and for a long moment, simply looked at her, his pale green eyes startling in the tanned face, his mobile mouth so promising.

Ducking her head to the horse, she said, "I wish I knew how to reach him," she confided. "Don't suppose you have the secret?"

A warning whispered through her mind. Roxanne's voice, the first day Zeke had come into the restaurant. *The woman that can tame him probably hasn't been born.*

Mattie would do well to remember that. More than once she'd caught herself thinking she might be the one that could do it. Not tame him, exactly. Gentle him, lead him home.

She needed to remember it very likely wasn't possible. If she chose to make love with him, that was all it would be. No roses and lace, as Zeke put it. No happy ending at the end of the road. Only memories of a time snatched like moonshine from the rest of her bland and ordinary life.

She wished she could decide if it would be worth it.

Brian and Vince made good time to Pagosa Springs. They settled in a motel and had a meal, then went through the phone book. Amanda Reeves had told them Zeke Shephard had some land nearby, but his name wasn't listed in the small telephone directory.

Discreet inquiries and descriptions yielded nothing. No one remembered a big man on a motorcycle, no one saw the woman. In frustration, his control near to snapping, Brian left Vince in the motel to try the telephone information services in the little towns all through the surrounding mountains, and went to a real estate office. A pretty young clerk sat behind the reception desk. Her dress was neat and pressed, but several years out of fashion, and she wore her hair in a decade's-old style. There were no rings on her fingers. "Hello," she said. "Can I help you?"

He gave her his best Sunday smile. "I hope so. I'm looking for someone—my natural brother. Adopted outside the family when he was three."

It was the right choice. The woman's face softened. "Sit down. What makes you think I can help you?"

Brian told his story.

* * *

George was a widower with three boys, ranging in age from thirteen to six. His grandmother, a woman who spoke in a mingling of Spanish and English, fixed them a huge lunch. Mattie and Zeke sat with the family and two hands from the barns.

And this, too, was an adventure, something she'd only read about: a ranch-house meal served at a huge kitchen table covered with a blue gingham cloth. From what she'd read, she expected fluffy biscuits or pot roast; instead, tortillas, chili, beans and shredded beef were served in the same staggering portions and downed with the same gusto. Mattie ate as much as any of them, her appetite heightened by the good mountain wind and the mouth-watering smell of the meat.

The thirteen-year-old flirted with her and the six-year-old bragged to her about his horse, which was bigger and better and smarter than all the other horses in the world. Mattie smiled in appreciation, winking at the older boy over his younger brother's head.

Zeke and George talked horses. Endlessly. The visit lasted three hours, and they were still talking horse-flesh when a thin line of clouds appeared on the western horizon. "We have to get back up the mountain," Zeke said with some regret. "It was sure good to talk, though."

Mrs. Romero halted by the stove. "Stay over a night, why don't you? Plenty of room."

"Well, I appreciate the offer, Miz Romero," Zeke said, standing, "but I've got to get my supplies in."

The woman's black eyes sparkled. "Ah. Okay, Zeke, but next time, you stay awhile. Give George some company."

"I'll do that."

She packed food into plastic containers and pressed the paper bag into Mattie's arms. "Good to see a young woman eat so well," she said with a wink. "Got to keep up your strength, eh?"

Mattie blushed, but thanked her.

And then they were back on their way up the mountain. "I think we're going to have a race on our hands," Zeke said. "Sorry about that. You might get wet again."

"It's no big deal. I'm not sugar. I won't melt."

But the air temperature dropped fast as they climbed and the clouds moved in. Mattie pressed close to Zeke's back, putting her arms around his waist and leaning against him. He touched her hands on his stomach once, as if to assure her he didn't mind.

The wind started to whip through the forest, buffeting them. Mattie felt Zeke's struggle to keep the bike under control in the face of that wind, felt the muscles in his whole body going into the fight. Once again, she was impressed by his physical strength.

Lightning cracked through the sky, bright and terrifying, companion thunder tearing across the clouds, and rain exploded from the sky in a torrent. "I'm gonna pull over," Zeke shouted.

Blinded by the driving rain when she lifted her head, Mattie ducked behind the shield of Zeke's shoulder. He pulled off the road and parked the bike under some trees, then grabbed Mattie's hand. "Run!"

He led, down a path on the mountainside, through the trees. Lightning flashed, thunder boomed and the rain pounded down upon them as they tumbled down the hill.

Mattie found it exhilarating. She felt as if she were flying, dancing over tree branches and rocks, skirting shrubs. She was soaked, but it didn't matter; she shook her head and tossed rain from her eyes and kept running. Her blood sizzled with the wild flashes of light and sound.

Near the foot of the hill by a stream, an outcropping of rock formed an open-sided cave. A single shelf of sandstone jutted out over the ground, creating a natural shelter. She and Zeke ducked under it.

Mattie laughed, wiping water from her face. There was such a wild exhilaration in her chest, she wanted to whoop. Beyond the sheltering rock, rain poured down in a misty gray curtain, furious and blinding. "Wow!" she cried. "That was great!"

Zeke made no response, and Mattie glanced over at him, wondering if he'd turned an ankle or something on the way down.

He stood there under the shelf of rock, his head nearly touching the ceiling. Water streamed over his hard-carved face, and his shirt clung to his beautiful flesh, outlining every rise of muscle, every curve of bone...everything.

His fists were clenched at his sides and Mattie saw the boiling was back in his eyes. This time, he didn't have to say it. Mattie knew.

A low, frustrated growl came from his throat. Mattie faced him squarely. "It wouldn't be so hard if you didn't fight it so much," she said.

His gaze skimmed over her body and Mattie realized her clothes were probably as invisible as his; her shirt was pale pink cotton, thin and worn. She could feel the way it clung to her breasts and waist. Nervously, she plucked at it.

His eyes were unreadable when they flickered back to her face. "It doesn't help."

Uncertainty filled her. Earlier, she'd felt very clear about wanting him, but his words at the ranch had shattered a little of her optimism. She didn't know how she'd feel if she let go with this man, didn't know if she could just walk away without regrets when it was all done.

"Having second thoughts, now, aren't you?"

Mattie looked away, shifted, feeling exposed and uncomfortable and unsure.

With one swift move, he grabbed her arm. "I think it's too late for second thoughts," he said, and Mattie looked up. She saw the blaze of wildness in his eyes, the dark hunger in his face, and she swayed toward him as he hauled her close—so close and hard against him.

His mouth was wet and hot and intensely demanding, so sharp and piercing with need that it broke through Mattie's defenses the way nothing else could have. A burst of excruciating hunger made her almost frantic with wanting him. She shifted in his arms and met his kiss wide open, giving as furiously as she took.

"Oh, Mattie," he said against her mouth. "I've never wanted a woman in my life like I want you. You're driving me crazy."

He kissed her chin, her throat, the half circle of flesh visible above her shirt. With one hand, he tugged her shirt from the top of her jeans and skimmed a hand beneath the fabric, roving upward.

Abruptly, he dropped to the ground, and dragged Mattie into his lap, kissing her as he tugged her shirt over her head. Mattie willingly lifted her arms, shivering when the wind touched her bare skin. Zeke groaned, and nestled them closer together, Mattie straddling him, her heat against his.

There was sureness in her movements, a sense of utter rightness. Without shame, she let him unclasp her bra and skim it down her arms, his hands coming back to circle and lift her breasts. A sound, dark and wordless, came from his throat as he touched her, no longer rushing. She watched his face as his fingers curled around her, as his thumbs traced a circle around her nipples. His beautiful face, so ravaged . . . her fingers curled against his cheeks, and he lifted his gaze to her, showing her the sultriness in the green irises as his hands teased and stroked her into a quivering she couldn't control. Over and over his thumbs skimmed her nipples, until they felt so rigid and engorged she was embarrassed.

Mattie thought she was the one in control, the one who was letting this happen, but Zeke didn't tremble now, and there was a sense of masterful orchestration in his movements, in the way he turned, still holding her gaze, and sucked her finger into his mouth, then let her go and bent his head to her breast.

She cried out as his mouth closed over one nipple, hot in contrast to the cold rain around them. Slow, slow, slow his mouth moved, suckling, then not, scraping and laving, his head only lifting to give the same attention to the other side.

Mattie's trembling increased until she could not control it. She clutched his shoulders. "Zeke," she cried softly, not knowing what she needed, how to stop the quaking in her limbs.

It was only then that she realized how remote he seemed. There was nothing specific, no change in his movements, but all at once, she felt as if she were being serviced rather than loved.

He reached between them to unsnap her jeans, and Mattie froze, suddenly aware that she didn't want this, not here, not like this. Not with him so cool and unemotional. She remembered the kiss he'd blown her back in Kismet—that aloof and cynical kiss—She grabbed his hands. "Stop."

He yanked her closer to him, pressing the rigid weight of his arousal against that aching place between her thighs. She bit back a moan, struggling to control the shaking in her body.

"You don't want to stop, Mattie," he said, but she didn't like his tone of voice. Too sure, too cocky. He moved himself against her and Mattie felt the answering rise of her body, a pulsing that began deep, deep inside.

"Damn you!" She shoved him away and stood up, crossing her arms over her naked breasts. She nearly stumbled in her haste, and scraped her upper arm on the wall. Furious and frustrated and trembling, she blindly looked for her shirt.

Zeke's lay in a heap near her foot and she grabbed it, instead, shaking the wet, tangled fabric and yanking it on as well as she could. "You're such a jerk!"

He didn't move, just knelt where he was, hands on his knees, looking savage and beautiful and as angry as she. His eyes blazed. "That's what I keep trying to tell you."

"I didn't ask for that." She clasped the shirt around her closely, folded her arms defensively.

"No, you're asking for a whole lot more, aren't you, Miss Mary?" He stood up and advanced toward her. "You want to lead me to the light. Or you want the bad boy you thought you saw out there in Kismet on motorcycle. You can't see me for me at all."

"You won't let me."

He loomed over her in the small space, tanned and untamed and bare-chested, all his scars showing plainly. "All you have to do is look, Mattie. I'm right here in front of you."

She stared at him, not quite understanding.

He touched her lips with his fingers, trailed his hand over her chin. "I've wanted you since the first time I saw you. Wanted that mouth—" he traced the curve of her lip "—and it's just what I thought it would be."

Miniscule trembling began anew as his hands dropped lower. "You think you're all covered up, don't you," he said and touched her breasts. "I can see straight through this shirt." Her nipple leaped to his touch and she backed away, right into the wall.

He leaned over her, putting his hands on either side of her head, bending over so his mouth hovered over hers. "I want you, Miss Mary," he said, his voice so low it almost didn't register. "I kept trying to tell myself to leave you alone, but things don't always work out the way we plan, do they?" He did that excruciating thing he'd done at the pool, rubbed his tongue over her bottom lip. She couldn't breathe. "I want you," he repeated, and nipped a little where his tongue had been, sending a sharp, delicious pain into her abdomen. "Slow and fine, wild and hot, and rightside up and upside down. Do you want me?"

Mattie reached for him, but he caught her hands. "Tell me."

The rain poured and thunder crashed. Mattie whispered, "I want you, Zeke."

He kissed her then, and it was honest and deep, with no holding back. "Then you can have me, Miss Mary. And I'm gonna have you." He lifted his head. "But it isn't going to be here or now."

She stared at him, acutely disappointed.

He tugged the shirt closed over her breasts. "I want you right, Mattie," he said. "If we do it here, we'll be freezing and have to climb into wet clothes and the ground will be too rough." He kissed her. "I want you right."

Mattie caught his hands. "Zeke—" she protested, but didn't know how to go on. She didn't know what to say or do. Her whole body felt as if it had been half plugged into an outlet, and she was neither on nor off.

"Say it, Mattie," he said. He lifted his hands from her body, but she could feel his heat so close. "What do you want?"

He kissed her, his tongue teasing the edges of her mouth. "Tell me and I'll tell you."

"Touch me," she whispered.

He brushed her shoulder. "Like that?"

"No," she whispered. She reached for him, no longer content to be led down whatever path it was he thought he had to take. She stroked his flat stomach and bent her head to his chest, kissing his flat nipple, trailing her tongue over the light, crisp hair on his chest.

She reached for the snap on his jeans. His huge hands seized her wrists. "Mattie, I'm serious. We'll be miserable if we don't wait."

"I'm going to be miserable if we do."

He touched her face. "Trust me."

Mattie sighed. Once again, she was going to miss out. "Fine," she said and went to sit in the corner to wait out the rain.

Chapter 13

Even without making love, the ride back to the cabin was unadulterated misery. The rain had slowed to a mild pattering sprinkle, but the wind sliced through their wet clothes with sharp, stinging needles of ice. Zeke felt his hair get stiff on his shoulders and knew Mattie had to feel even worse. She'd never been stuck in a rainstorm on a motorcycle before.

The alternative had been to stay in the cave by the stream and freeze slowly. Even with a fire, they would have grown more and more miserable. Better to cut their losses and get back as quickly as possible.

The misery, however, did perform the necessary duty of quenching the fierce desire between them. Not even Zeke felt randy by the time they got back. He sent Mattie in ahead while he unfastened their groceries from the back of the bike. "Get out of those wet clothes and start some water boiling."

She nodded mutely. With a stab of guilt, Zeke saw her lips were pale blue.

He gave her a few minutes, then hauled in the supplies. Her clothes were in a wet pile on the floor, and she huddled on the bed, shivering, wrapped in his stallion blanket. "I'm sorry, Mattie," he said, dropping the pack. His own teeth chattered and he kicked off his boots. "Go on down to the sauna. I'll bring towels and coffee in a minute."

"That's okay, Zeke. I'll get warm in a minute."

"Not like that you won't," he returned, stripping off his shirt and rubbing his flesh with a towel. "Go on. The sauna will make you feel better. That's why I have it."

Reluctantly, she sat up. "Can I take the blanket in with me?"

"Yeah." He had a spare sleeping bag in the crawl space.

Clutching the blanket around her, she hobbled out.

Zeke shed his soggy jeans and wrapped himself in a big terry-cloth robe. Barefooted and chilled to the bone, he made two big mugs of instant coffee, put generous helpings of sugar and powdered cream into Mattie's, and carried them outside.

It was gloomy and dark because of the heavy clouds, which showed no signs of clearing out. Unusual for afternoon storms to last, but it did happen sometimes.

He knocked on the sauna door. Mattie called, "Come in," and he entered.

Curled in the blanket, covered to her nose, she sat on the low bench. The perpetual fire was low and the room was not terribly warm yet.

He gave her the coffee. "It'll warm you up from the inside."

One white arm slipped from between the folds of the blanket to take the cup. "I've never been so bone-cold in my entire life."

"I know, honey." He touched her shoulder. "It'll be better in a little while. I'll get some more wood."

From the pile of wood outside, Zeke selected slender bits of kindling and carried them inside to get the fire going well again. While the smaller pieces caught and began to burn, he gathered another armload and took it inside, closing the door firmly behind him as the rain began to fall again with a vengeance. "Albuquerque low," he commented, feeding the fire some healthier logs.

"Pardon me?"

He poked the embers and watched the kindling begin to flicker. Yellow flames started to lick at the logs. "It's a weather pattern that makes storms just hang over the mountains. We'll probably have rain for a day or two now. Good thing we got supplies today."

"I suppose it is." Her hair was beginning to dry in the little wisps around her cheeks that he found so appealing. Her days in the sunshine had given her a burnished look—her skin warming, her hair taking on hints of sunny color. Feeling a stir in his thawing nether regions, he tied his robe more tightly and sat on the wooden floor by the pool.

Overhead, the rain pattered down, a relaxing sound that provided a comfortable counterpoint to the crackling fire. A smell of pine rose to mingle with the musky scent of the water, and the combination caused him to lean back against the wall. "I love this place," he said.

"Me, too," Mattie said quietly. "I was thinking when I was in here last night that I've never been anywhere that was so welcoming."

"Starting to thaw a little now?"

She smiled. "A little." One bare foot snuck out of the blanket. "Surely you don't ride that bike in the wintertime."

"I have a truck in storage in town." He sipped the hot coffee, his own innards feeling vaguely human again. "Ready for steam?"

"Sure."

He bent over the pool and splashed the incinerator. The steam was poor quality, but it wouldn't be much longer before they could engulf themselves in it if they wanted to. He splashed again and heard a satisfying sizzle.

"What made you think of building this?" Mattie asked. Her other foot had emerged from the blanket, and both legs hung over the bench now, naked to the knee. Zeke wondered if she'd put on dry clothes or just wrapped the blanket around her naked body.

"There's a hot-springs resort a little farther north," he said. "They had one like this up there." To distract himself from the delectable vision of those slender, bare calves, he tossed up more water. Steam floated down around them.

"We'll need the lantern before much longer." He leaned to give her a book of matches from his robe pocket. "It's right behind you on that hook."

When she leaned forward, the blanket slipped away from her shoulder and he saw that it was bare. As if she didn't notice his suddenly intense perusal, she set her coffee on the bench beside her and adjusted the blanket so that it was tucked under her arms, remov-

ing all doubt about whether she wore anything beneath.

Anchoring the blanket firmly over her breasts, she
lit the lantern. There was one bad moment when he
thought her covering might slip all the way off, but it
stayed secure and she yanked it up casually when she
finished her task.

The pale yellow light tumbled over her, gleaming
along one shoulder and arm, disappearing in the seductive hollow between her breasts, skirting the edge
of the blanket to fall on her foot.

Zeke averted his gaze.

The fire roared and the rain poured. Zeke's body
came all the way unfrozen and reminded him of what
he'd been in the middle of when the weather and lo-
cation had intervened. He wondered if Mattie still
wanted him the way he wanted her. She seemed to be
sending no signals his way; in fact, she seemed quite
content to just sit there, sipping coffee.

He told himself it would be best to leave it alone. Let
her go. Something happened to him when he touched
her, something he didn't know if he liked. He came all
undone.

Restlessly, he reached for the small wooden cup
floating in the pool and tossed a solid spray of water
at the incinerator. Thick soothing steam enveloped
them.

Not that it helped much. The delectable Mattie
closed her eyes and leaned back against the wall. The
position showed off that long, beautiful throat, and
Zeke gazed at it hungrily, watching as steam dewed her
flesh. Lamplight glowed over the edge of her collarbone, spilled on the plump tops of her breasts, round
and glowing with moisture.

He shifted irritably, hard as a scratching post.

At the cave, he'd felt something evil come over him when she'd expectantly let him take her shirt and bra from her body. It was the same thing that came over him when he ruined his past relationships, something dark he couldn't control, that turned him into a world-class jerk.

Usually, however, he did wait until he got laid.

A cynical voice spoke deep within his mind. Nice try.

The truth was, Zeke—for the first time in his life—was vulnerable to a woman. There she had been, sturdy and strong and ripe, naked to the waist in the great outdoors, hungry for his touch—and Zeke had been pierced clear through with the knowledge that this was no ordinary woman. That this time, he might be the one to fall, the one who ended up wanting more than she could give.

He didn't know what would happen to him if he let himself go. It wasn't the blistering need he feared anymore, either. Not the sex.

He feared for his heart. He didn't know how she'd done it, but somehow she'd slipped through all the defenses he'd built over the years, and he didn't know what would happen if he let his guard down enough to make love.

He glanced at her again. How could he resist?

Had the blanket slipped a little lower or was that wishful thinking? A little more of her leg showed now, there was no doubt about that. He could see the vulnerable flesh of her inner thigh just above her knee. What would she do if he eased over there and kissed that place?

Into the long silence, Mattie said, "Penny for your thoughts."

He jerked his gaze up. "What?"

"Penny for your thoughts," she said again, and there was a spark of mischief in her eyes. She lifted her coffee cup and the blanket did slip this time, almost all the way down. It hung tantalizingly at the edge of her breasts, ready to fall away the next time she took a breath.

Damn.

He put down his coffee cup deliberately. Gathering the robe around his thighs, he stepped into the shallow pool and waded over to her. "I'm thinking it's time, now, Miss Mary."

With a wide-eyed gaze, she stared at him. "Is it?"

He reached for the edge of the blanket and slipped a hand below it. As he'd known it would, the fabric tumbled from her breasts, from her body, fell around her nakedness like the shed shell of a newly born wood nymph.

He groaned and swayed forward to kiss her throat, brushing her breasts with his hands. Her limbs were trembling again as he let his mouth descend, let his mouth burn a trail over her breasts and belly and secret heat, over a slim white thigh to that vulnerable place on the inside of her knee. He paused there and bit her lightly. She made a low, pained sound and tugged at his robe. Zeke stepped back to shake it off, caring little that it was soaked as he dragged it through the water.

Mattie reached for him. "Let me touch you," she whispered, sliding forward until she could join him, face-to-face in the small pool. She spread her palms open on his chest and touched him all over, smoothing his chest and arms, his hips and buttocks and belly.

But they'd waited too long for much play. When she took his heat into her hand, he groaned and captured her small naked form against him. Dragging the blanket from the bench to the floor, he lifted her from the pool and lay her down on the thin soft pallet.

He covered her with himself, and struggling for control, trapped her between his legs and arms, stretching her arms over her head to kiss her hard. Mattie lifted her head and kissed him back, furiously, a soft, panting noise coming from her throat. The sound brought the savagery to him again, that wild, demonic need to possess her. He moved his body against hers to feel her breasts and the tantalizing whisper of her female heat against his raging organ.

In spite of the mark it would leave, he suckled her neck, and heard the low, aroused sound in her throat intensify. He bent his head over her breasts and tasted her nipples, using his tongue to bring that writhing to a fever pitch. She arched upward, pressing herself into him, asking the thing he wanted most to give.

He let her arms go and kissed her belly. Mattie dragged him up to her, to kiss him, deeply and hungrily. His control came undone. With a pained groan, he shifted and she accommodated him eagerly, parting her legs, offering herself.

The kissing was too much, too intimate, he thought. He should stop kissing her. But her mouth was like a potent spell—the more he drank, the more he needed. He couldn't stop. He clasped her soft breast in his hand and held her lips and eased his manhood into her wet and waiting heat. Oh, just a little at a time, just a little, so he wouldn't hurt her.

But she arched suddenly, shifting her body to bring him home, and Zeke groaned at the searing pleasure of being fully sheathed in Mattie. Mattie.

Then there was no thought. He grabbed her shoulders and thrust, feeling her rise and swell and whimper as they moved in ways not simple or easy or calm, only purely, desperately hungry.

As they moved, he felt the earth shift around him, as if his place in the universe had been suddenly changed. He looked down at Mattie's face, and even in the midst of his passion, he was overwhelmed with details—the fan of her long eyelashes over her sunkissed cheeks, the spray of her hair on her ear, the perfection of her long white throat—and it didn't feel like anything he'd known before.

He kissed her and kissed her and kissed her, moving in her mouth and in her body, overcome with a painful rippling sense of rightness. She began to quiver, lost, and clutched his shoulders fiercely.

He lifted his head and slowed down, kissing her gently now, drawing out her pleasure. Not to illustrate his prowess, but because he could see by the wonder in her face this was a new sensation, that she'd not made acquaintance with her body this way before. His breath came in heavy, uneven rasps, but he held on, teasing her mouth with his tongue, touching her breasts with his hands, letting that power build and build and build—

She came apart, and Zeke let go, driving into her without restraint, thrilling to the cry that escaped her throat. Her body convulsed around him, a roaring filled his ears.

He splintered into a billion pieces.

His heart, made of thinnest glass, shattered.

And rather than look into her face, rather than let her know what she'd done, he waited until the pulsing of her body was finished, until his was done, and eased away. He didn't look at her, only stood up and went out into the rain to hide.

At first, Mattie was stunned. Her body still rippled with the power of their joining. She was not a virgin, but she might as well have been for the difference she felt in herself now. His departure left her cold, but worse than that, she felt as if he'd taken a part of her—ripped away a shard of her soul as he stood up and ran into the rain.

Behind the shock came anger, pure and white, filling every corner and unknown cranny of her mind. She jumped up and grabbed the blanket to wrap around her and stormed outside.

Rain blinded her momentarily, and the ground was muddy beneath her feet. Clutching the blanket around her newly warm body, she shivered at the press of rain, looking around for Zeke. He was nowhere in sight.

She paused, frowning, hoping she wouldn't lose this anger before she found him. It was about time he got a piece of her mind for this on-and-off, hot-and-cold nonsense. Did men think women were immune to sexual feelings? That they could just turn them off at will?

An odd sound of water reached her, not the rain. She listened carefully and remembered the shower.

She rounded the small building and saw him standing under the warm water of the outdoor shower, his hair soaked once again by a combination of rain and shower water. His skin shimmered with pearlescent light, the last breath of day seeming to concentrate here, on him, on the long limbs corded with muscle, on the lean lines of his scarred and beautiful back, on his buttocks and thighs and calves, on his bent head and rigidly clasped fists.

He looked—broken.

Her anger dissolved instantly. Dragging her soaked blanket with her, she went to him, dropping her covering when she reached the platform. Without a word, she joined him in the hot-and-cold water pouring down upon them, pressed her body against his back and put her arms around his body. The thick puckered scar pressed into her ear and she turned her face to kiss it.

He turned, big as a bear, and kissed her. Now she tasted desperation, a lostness as gray as the day, and she held him close, stroking his arms and his face, touching his chest. Slowly, feeling his need, she explored his body with her lips and her hands—the lean ropy arms and broad chest, his hard waist, the silky, pointed weight of his manhood. And when he was groaning, clutching her hair, she kissed him again. He lifted her easily, bracing her on the edge of the rail, and drove himself into her with a fury that had nothing to do with violence and everything to do with love.

She loved him. The thought came to her in the aftermath, with her head nestled on his shoulder, her legs wrapped easily around his waist, his arms locked around her back. Rain poured around them softly and Mattie felt as if it were washing away everything. The past. The future. The false starts and false messages and false fronts each had erected against the other. It poured over them, salty and fresh and clean.

At last, Zeke moved, lifting his head to look at her. So serious. She touched his face. "What pagans we are," she said softly.

"Yeah." The word was thick with satisfaction. He looked up at the rain and closed his eyes, his hands still wrapped around her back. Mattie knew with an acute awareness that she would always remember this moment: both of them nude in the falling twilight of a mountain summer, sated and yet still hungry, Zeke's strong face tipped to received the gift of rain, his broad hands warm on her. She lifted her own face to it, feeling again the strange sense of power that had come upon her in this shower once before, only this time it was stronger, wilder—she was the trees and the rain and Zeke and herself all at once.

He kissed her suddenly and scooped her into his arms. "We're going to catch our death of cold out here. I'm also starving."

"What are we going to wear back to the house? Everything is soaked."

"We'll walk. Like Adam and Eve."

"Don't you ever get visitors up here?"

"Never. Not even once." He looked down at her. "You're the first human who's ever seen the place."

"What about the propane man?"

"He won't be here till tomorrow."

"I still feel weird walking all over creation with no clothes on."

"Then let's run." He grabbed her hand and with a shriek, Mattie ran after him, sure at any moment someone would drive up the road, or a helicopter would fly over. He seemed to have no such worries.

They dashed inside and both dived for the bed, grabbing the sleeping bag to cover themselves in.

Damp, laughing, they gravitated toward each other. Nestled in warmth, they slept.

Chapter 14

Brian cursed the rain. The Pagosa Springs records had no listing for Zeke Shephard. The woman there referred him to Creede. He located the small town on the map and tamped down his frustration. It was another ninety or a hundred miles, over twisting, high mountain roads.

Thanking the woman cheerfully, he returned to the motel where Vince watched reruns of *I Love Lucy* on the small television. "We've gotta go," he said.

"In this?" Vince pointed to the pouring gray rain falling beyond the windows. "You must be outta your mind."

"Rain or no rain, we've got to find that bitch. Two days I've got to get this right, or it's your life and mine, Vincent." He flipped off the television. "Get moving."

"Bri, have you ever driven mountain roads?"

"No. Have you?"

"Not until this trip. You notice how narrow they are, how wide that El Camino is?" He gestured to the window. "Now they'll be slick, too. It's suicide to get out in this mess."

"Move," Brian said without flickering an eyebrow.

Vince slitted his eyes. "What are you gonna do if I say I ain't gonna do it?"

It was the last rebellion in a very long list. Brian pulled the revolver from his shoulder holster. "I'll kill you," he said without emotion.

Vince eyed the weapon with pursed lips. No fear flickered over the sallow face. "It ain't worth dying over," he said at last, picking up the keys.

After a time, Mattie stirred awake. The cabin was cool and dim, lit only by the lantern. Zeke held her close, his big arms draped heavily over her shoulders. For a moment, his huge, engulfing presence was startling, but her memory seeped back. The sauna. The shower. She blushed, thinking of the run back up the hill.

She had no desire to move just yet, and because his hand hung in full view, she touched it. An enormous, long-fingered hand, tanned with his outdoor pursuits, strong with the work he did. His nails were short and flat and oval.

Working hands. The incidents of a lifetime showed there. New little scrapes—one on his middle knuckle, another tiny cut by one fingernail. She glimpsed a callus on his palm.

And there on the wrist, where the flesh was thinnest, most sensitive, was a perfectly round, whitish scar. Old. Almost faded.

Mattie brushed her thumb over the lingering reminder of the brutality Zeke had faced as a child. There were probably a dozen or more on his body, each one the imprint of a cigarette cruelly held to young flesh in punishment.

The average person had trouble imagining how a father could repeatedly, deliberately inflict such pain on a child, Mattie knew. She forgave them the inability, because it meant most people were too compassionate to allow that such horror existed.

Mattie had seen it. Not always this kind of brutality, not always even physical. In her tenure in foster homes, she'd found good people, kind people, and she'd found a brutal one. She'd also heard the stories of the other children in the homes—most who were not orphans, like Mattie, but wards of the state because their parents had so neglected or abused them. Horrible stories.

She traced the lines on his thumb, touched the flat nail. For all that she had suffered loss, her first six years had been spent in the bosom of a mother and father who loved her—and after seeing the homes many a child was born to, it was something she'd learned to be grateful for.

Zeke stirred. "What are you thinking about?" he said sleepily.

"My parents."

His fingers curled around her hand. "Do you remember them?"

Mattie brushed away the mists of time and called up the picture she carried of her mother. "A little. It's more of a feeling of warmth, smells, snips of things."

"Tell me."

"My mother smelled of lilacs. Lilac dusting powder. And she had really long, pretty hair." One memory was clear—her mother combing Mattie's hair, even then very long, to her waist. "My dad worked at a newspaper as a printer. I remember this pungent odor of ink and sweat and cigarette smoke. He had a flat-top haircut."

Zeke touched her hair. "I still like it this way," he said. "It suits you."

Mattie shifted in his arms. "You never saw it long."

"True. Bet you hid behind it."

She chuckled at this accuracy. "I miss it most when I wish I could duck behind something. Very convenient."

It was dark in the room and a chill had begun to seep through the walls. "I'm hungry. Are you?"

"Starving," Zeke said. "How about if you get something heated up and I'll go get some firewood and start a fire?"

"Okay."

He kissed her, lingeringly. "Don't get too well dressed," he said in that dark voice, brushing a palm over her belly.

A warm ripple passed through her. "You either."

He climbed over her and stretched mightily, comfortable with his nude body in the way only a well-made man could be. His hair had dried in a tumble of waves on his broad, powerful shoulders, and Mattie admired the muscled length of his back, new desire stirring within her.

He shifted to tug a clean pair of jeans from a drawer, and the light of the lantern he'd lit caught the puckered scar on his back. "How did you get that scar, Zeke?"

Without looking at her, he lazily donned his jeans. "Which one?"

Intrigued by his tone, which was wary but not closed, she said, "Pick one."

He tossed her a long thermal T-shirt. "Get my supper going, woman. I'm starving." As Mattie sat up to put it on, he dived for her, tumbling her backward in the bed, kissing her tummy and breasts.

Mattie laughed, almost deliriously happy. She tickled him. "Get up, you big lug! I'm starving, too!"

He lifted his head and his eyes shone. "That's how women stay around me."

She lifted her head to kiss him and fell back, smiling. "Go get some wood so we don't freeze."

"If I tell you dark stories, there's a price," he said. "Is it weird?"

He laughed. "No." He got up. "But you might not like it."

"I'll take my chances."

Curled on the braided rug before a roaring fire, they ate canned chili and biscuits from a mix that required only water. It was the best meal of Mattie's life.

Afterward, they made love again. Lazily, without the edge of frantic and painful need that had marked their joining earlier. Now they took time to explore, talking softly, touching, playing, unfolding to each other.

As they lay together in the warmth of that unfolding, Mattie felt again the puckered scar on his back. "Tell me the story of this one," she said quietly.

He shifted, to lean his head on his hand. He smiled. "Othello is responsible for that one."

"What happened?"

"I was trying to break him and he wasn't taking kindly to the process. He threw me and I smashed into a gate of the corral. Broke my arm in two places, and the gate latch just about tore my heart out from the back."

She shuddered. "And you got right back on, didn't you?"

"Well, not right away. It took me a month or two to get back on my feet, but we did come to an understanding eventually."

"What understanding?"

He grinned. "I'm the boss."

Made bold by his ready answer, she touched the thin white line by his mouth. "This one?"

He frowned, but it wasn't a brooding expression. He touched the place and blinked. "You know, I can't remember. I'm sure my dad did it, but I don't remember the circumstances."

"And this?" She touched his wrist.

"Cigarettes." He brushed his hand over his torso, indicating the others. "All of the little round ones are cigarettes. It was what he used when I interfered."

There was a lot less growling in his voice than there had been the first time. In fact, he told it matter-of-factly, as if it were all water under the bridge, which she knew wasn't true.

"How did you interfere?"

To her surprise, he grinned. "Same way I have been since you showed up, Miss Mary." He smoothed a lock of hair from her face. "It seems to be a habit of mine. Back then, I put myself between him and my sisters."

"That was brave."

His mouth turned down at the corners. "Nah. They didn't have anybody else."

"Neither did you."

"I was stronger."

And Mattie saw in the pale green depths of his gaze the truth of that statement. For all that he'd suffered, he'd survived. Almost whole.

"Where are your sisters now? Do you ever see them?"

"No," he said. "Not for a while now. They all pretty much still live in Mississippi. One's a lawyer in Jackson, the rest are just your garden-variety married ladies."

"Six?"

He shook his head. "Only five sisters. One hung herself when I ran away that time, got my tattoo."

There was another door, one closed so long cobwebs hung all around it. Mattie knew, looking into his eyes, that he felt responsible in some way for that death. "So you go around rescuing strangers to make up for it."

He lifted an eyebrow. "I reckon."

"Do you have a lot of nieces and nephews?"

"None of us have had children."

Mattie let that slide, too, sensing it led places he wouldn't want to walk. And what more light would be shed, anyway? His father must have been a brutal, brutal man.

"So how," she said lightly, "did you get to be so good with babies?"

"My mama has a lot of family. I probably had, oh, at least twenty, twenty-five first cousins." He lifted a shoulder. "Even when I was little, I liked the little ones. They don't talk back and don't ask a lot. Just love. Used to like to make 'em laugh. It was so easy.''

"All that family and no one came to your rescue." The words were out of her mouth before she could stop them.

"Not all families are like the Waltons, Mattie."

"But someone had to be kind to you somewhere, Zeke, or you wouldn't be the man you are."

"I had my sisters. We had one another. It's a lot."

Mattie thought of the cursory way most of the men of her acquaintance treated children. Most of them were afraid of babies. It seemed a cruel twist of fate that he would not have any of his own. Almost unnatural.

"Don't do it, Miss Mary," he said. "I see those rose-colored glasses you're putting on. Don't do it." He squeezed her shoulder for emphasis. "I am who I am."

Mattie looked at him, a deep pinch in her chest.

He touched her mouth, kissed her forehead, rested his hand on her stomach. "This is real nice, Mattie, but it isn't gonna last. Don't think it will."

She swallowed the sorrow his words gave her and reached for him wordlessly, pressing her face into his warm, hair dusted chest, wishing there was something she could do, something she could say, to make him see—

See what? That she was the right woman for him? That she could give him the love he'd never had? That she could give him children to ease the past?

All those things.

But he could not accept such a gift and Mattie would not cause him more pain by extending it. "I know, Zeke," she said against his chest. "I know."

He held her tight, his hand clasping her head to him, his lips in her hair.

In the morning, Zeke made coffee. Mattie still slept, the sleeping bag tucked over her breasts, held close like that teddy bear she wouldn't leave behind in her burning house. In the gilded light of morning, he could see the scars on her hands plainly, the rough, darkened skin over her knuckles, a couple of places where the flesh seemed stretched too tight.

They weren't marring scars and she seemed not to think about them. Not the way Zeke did about his. He was fairly sure children had teased her, as they had teased him, or given her those long pitying glances that were even worse.

Watching her sleep, he wondered where she got her strength. She was like a willow branch, bending easily on the rough currents of her life, doing what was required without whining or wincing. Losing her hair had to have been a major trauma—and yet she'd had the courage to cut it off. She'd done what had to be done.

On her long throat were the marks of his mouth, the savage marks he'd made on purpose, if he were honest, because he wanted to have some claim. It was juvenile, but there it was. No woman in his entire life stirred the kind of possessive, wild need he felt for her.

He wasn't the kind of man who thought himself in love often. There had been the painful, searing bit of first love when he was sixteen, but that had been it. Her family had moved away, and Zeke had joined the rodeo circuit as soon as he was able. Women were plentiful, and he learned early on how to give them what they wanted without giving up anything of himself.

For the most part, it worked. Every so often, he tangled with an Amanda, a woman who was bound and determined to housebreak him. Amanda had been the only one to extract vengeance, but there had doubtless been others who'd wanted to.

He felt no guilt. He told all of them he wasn't the settling-down kind. Made it clear from the beginning that he wanted nothing to do with commitments, picket fences or—especially—babies. After his telling them that, if they still took him on as a personal challenge, just who was to blame?

He'd started this with Mattie just the same way. Clear. Up front.

But this thing had been muddy right from the beginning. On day one, he'd started breaking his rules, the elaborate network of regulations he'd set for himself a long time ago.

In the big bed, Mattie shifted but didn't wake. He could see most of her back the way she lay, and knew a sudden longing to kiss each tiny bone of her spine, all the way down to those generous hips.

He smiled sleepily, thinking of her unbridled passion. If anyone had told him two weeks ago that Miss Mary would make love outside, standing up, in a rainstorm, he'd have laughed.

Which only went to prove he knew less about good girls than he thought. Because she was: good, honest, upright and trustworthy. And a hellcat in bed. What more could a man want? That angel face hid the most delicious wickedness.

He sighed and rubbed a hand over his face, ignoring the insistent thrust of his overworked parts. She had to be sore by now. He wouldn't bother her again.

The whole thing was out of control. *He* was out of control. He'd broken every rule he had. The first one about good girls. His second most important and never ignored: wear a condom at all times. Truth was, he'd gone into the drugstore for them yesterday and decided he'd avoid temptation if he didn't have one. Or Mattie would stop him.

So much for that idea.

He had rules about what he could tell about himself, too. To women friends, he'd occasionally let the story of his childhood come out; he knew wounds festered if they never saw the light. But he didn't tell that story to the women he slept with—the body/emotion link would get too strong.

He didn't let himself stay in emotionally dangerous situations, either. And yet, instead of finding ways to get Mattie away from him, he'd found a hundred ways to keep her here—against her protests.

He swore under his breath.

All those rules were in place for a reason, for protection, to keep him safe from emotional ties. He couldn't stand being vulnerable to anyone, ever.

But looking at Mattie O'Neal in his bed, he knew he was vulnerable to her. Even more so because she'd never ask for anything for herself. She loved him. She wanted to tell him that, and yet she hadn't. Not out of self-preservation, but to spare *him*.

There was a pounding ache in his heart, filling his chest. Another rule was that he would come here by himself, so he'd never get used to the feeling of having someone around, so loneliness would feel like solitude. As long as no other living, breathing human shared the space, the illusion was possible.

He would miss her when she was gone.

It was this last thought that propelled him across the room to her side, made him slide beneath the covers, jeans and all, and take her warm, soft body into his arms. She stirred sleepily, but did not awaken. Zeke was glad of it. She'd see too much in this moment. Far more than he wanted to show.

As if she were made of pieces torn from him, she flowed into his arms, her curves filling hollows, her heat covering his cold, her cheek fitting his shoulder exactly.

He closed his eyes and let himself feel her, knowing it was a pleasure that could not last.

They ate breakfast on the porch. Mattie kept hoping the raccoon would come, but he didn't. As they drank the last of the coffee, Zeke said, "Mattie."

She looked at him, alarmed by the dull tone of his voice. She said nothing, just waited for the other shoe.

A tic jumped by his right eye, near the scar. "You have to turn yourself in. I can't keep you safe here and you can't hide forever."

She opened her mouth to protest. He held up a hand, turning to lean on the rough table between them. "Listen, all right? All the way through."

Something wary and tired about him made her do as he asked. "I'm listening," she said.

"The reward is for twenty-five thousand dollars, Mattie. If your information leads to Brian's arrest, you'll get the money."

"I don't care about the money."

"I know, but you ought to. Twenty-five thousand clams would go a long way to building whatever kind of future you want for yourself, so you don't have to depend on some job you hate or the security of a husband."

"I'm a very simple woman," she replied. "I don't need the money."

He sighed. "Then for one minute, I want you to think about what will happen if you don't testify and old Brian Murphy gets off scot-free. Now, the people he killed probably had mothers and wives and maybe even kids, and they deserve some justice... And I want you to think about what's going to happen five years from now, when Brian relaxes. When he's got all his ducks in a row again. And he looks around for another sweet girl to marry."

A small wave of dizziness passed through her. This was a possibility she'd never considered.

"What if she's not as lucky as you were and she goes ahead and marries him and has a couple of kids. Who's gonna lose when she does find out? Or when she doesn't find out and they come and take him away to jail for the rest of his life? Who loses?"

Mattie bent her head, ashamed that her fear had overridden her ability to think about the consequences of her actions on people other than herself and Brian.

"Your boyfriend and his crony wouldn't be looking for you if the police had anything else to go on, Mattie."

She stood up abruptly. "All right!" she shouted. "All right. I'll do it. But you take the money and buy Othello back. You make the call and have the police come get me here."

"Mattie, that's ridiculous. You need the money—it's you making the sacrifice."

"I don't want you to have the money for you, Zeke. Othello loves you."

Hurt, afraid, angry, Mattie slammed the chair into place under the table and stormed into the cabin.

Chapter 15

In the Creede surveyor's office, Brian hit pay dirt. Zeke Shephard had purchased eighty acres of mountain land four years before. Brian found the lot numbers on a map, then traced the roads. It might be a little bit tricky to find entrance, but they were close now.

Mattie O'Neal would be a corpse by sunset.

Mattie sat on the bed, her back propped against the wall, her legs crossed, watching Zeke get ready to go. "You don't want to come with me?" he asked.

"I'll just wait here. Get my things together."

He took his keys from the table. "Suit yourself. I'll be back in an hour or so. I'll call from the tackle shop down the road."

"Fine."

"Mattie, you don't have to do this alone. I'll go in with you, make sure you're taken care of. I'll even show up in court if you want me to."

She gazed at him impassively. "No."

For an instant, he met that gaze, his face reflecting nothing. Finally, he shrugged and grabbed his helmet. Without a word, he went out the front door and Mattie heard the bike start up and roar down the hill.

With a peculiar pain, she gazed around the room. They'd only been here three days. Two weeks ago, Mattie had never seen Zeke Shephard. A little over a month ago, she'd been living a quiet life as a secretary.

No wonder she felt dizzy.

But in many ways, this had always been the pattern of her life. Upheaval. Change. She'd become comfortable in a foster home, and find herself in another one, just that fast.

A person could get used to almost anything.

Resigned, she began to gather her things together, stuffing socks and rumpled clothes into her duffel bag without much thought. She had no idea where the police would take her, where she'd spend the night or live her life the next few weeks. Her apartment was likely still waiting for her. Her job was less certain.

The thought of returning to Kansas City sent a rigid, screaming resistance through her. She knew too much to go back. She'd seen another kind of life, and she wanted it.

Settling her book of poetry on top of the rest, she tugged the drawstring closed. She still had some gum and crackers to tide her over. Of the two hundred and thirty-three dollars she had taken with her from Kismet, more than two hundred remained. Enough to get her out of Kansas City once her business there was finished.

Zeke had left the door open upon his departure, and a soft wind blew over the threshold, calling to her. It carried a warm scent of drying pine needles and the song of birds. Seduced, Mattie wandered out to the bright summer morning and gazed around her in wonder. From the front of the cabin, the wide vistas of the valley were no longer visible and Mattie let her gaze wander up the mountainside, to the trees and stony outcroppings. The wind that had seduced her outside now caressed her face. She closed her eyes and lifted her chin, letting it blow away the tightness in her shoulders, the achy feeling in her chest.

Even now, knowing the brief, exciting, enthralling days she'd stolen with Zeke were over, she felt a promise in that wind. A sense of expectation, a sense of deliverance.

That was what she'd felt with Zeke. Deliverance. It was the unfulfilled promise of it that hurt so much this morning.

Last night, she had believed she'd broken through to the real Zeke, to the man who hid inside the shell. Even after he said there was no future for them, even when he warned her to take off her rose-colored glasses and insisted he'd ruin whatever came up between them, Mattie had only half believed him.

That was her own foolishness, though. It had nothing to do with Zeke. He played by his rules and Mattie had known what they were.

Thinking back to that morning in the Kismet diner when she had first seen him, it seemed impossible it had only been two weeks. He had changed her life.

If only she'd been able to do the same for him.

A glimmer of light on the side of the mountain caught her eye, and with a grin, she shaded her eyes with one hand. It was the hot spring! She hadn't realized it was visible from here, and she supposed it wasn't, unless you knew it was there.

Suddenly, she dashed back inside and dumped the contents of her tote bag on the bed. She tossed off her clothes, and quickly slipped into a pair of shorts and a loose T-shirt. Zeke said he'd be gone an hour or so. She'd just go take a dip in that pool while she waited for his return. It certainly beat brooding.

Unfortunately, walking proved conducive to thinking, too. As she followed the slim path up the hill, she remembered the hike with Zeke and his great pleasure in showing her the pool he'd dug. She thought of the way he felt in front of her on the bike, and the way his eyes could lighten to that brilliant pale emerald when he was teasing.

When she reached the pool, she remembered the way he had kissed her here, so desperately hungry, with such wild need.

God, she would miss him!

Was it possible to fall in love in so short a time—or was she just dazzled by the presence and size and sheer charisma of him? She had, after all, thought herself in love with Brian. Now she barely thought of him at all.

Would the same thing happen a few months from now when she thought back on Zeke? She didn't know. She didn't see how it was possible that she'd ever stop thinking about him. It felt incomplete, for one thing. She had learned only a tiny part of him, and wanted to know everything. All the things it would take a lifetime to learn.

Annoyed with her brooding, she waded into the pool.

How did a person ever answer these questions? She tipped back and floated in the warm, buoyant water, staring at the blazing Colorado sky above her. At last she found respite from the whirl of her thoughts. Floating in the mineral water that reminded her of Zeke, and smelled of earth and musk and the elements, she emptied her mind and simply floated between the bowl of the sky and ground below.

Until the wind carried the sound of Zeke's motorcycle to her. She scrambled up and swam to the far side of the pool, finding a toehold in a rock below the water so she could see the driveway in front of the cabin. When he parked the bike and cut the engine, Mattie cupped her hands around her mouth and called his name. He paused, looking around perplexed for a moment.

"Up here!" Mattie yelled. When he glanced up, she waved. He lifted a hand and moved toward the path that led to the pool.

Mattie watched him cross the clearing with long-limbed ease, his movements loose and calm. His hair shone in the sunlight. Her heart caught. Strider.

Yes, she loved him. It wasn't logical or sensible or anything of those other things. He was not the kind of man she'd daydreamed about all of her life, safe and stolid and dependable, but he was the one. The One.

When he emerged from the bend around a boulder a few minutes later, the pinching in her chest trebled, expanded, stole her breath.

Safe and solid and dependable were not the words most women would use to describe Zeke Shephard. They'd see his tattoo and wild hair and his big mean motorcycle and words like *sexy* and *exciting* and *dangerous* would come to mind. Mattie knew, because they'd been in her mind.

He *was* sexy. And exciting and vivid. But it was the dizzying combination of exciting and safe that made him dangerous, not anything inherent in him, just that simple fact that he would always protect and care for the small and defenseless, the babies and children and beleaguered women of the world.

As he stood on the edge of the pool, Mattie saw something else. In his beautiful, deep eyes, she saw how much the loss of her company would cost him. He looked like a man whose dog had just been hit by a truck.

It nearly broke her heart. He needed her, wanted her as much as he ever had, but last night they'd grown too close. To protect himself, to survive, he thought he had to push her away.

He needed her, and she knew nothing on earth would make him admit it.

She stared at him without speaking, letting that painful knowledge reverberate in her chest, and finally said, "Is it done?"

"Yeah." He kicked a rock on the edge of the pool. "They'll be coming for you shortly."

Mattie nodded. "I guess I'd better get out and get ready, then."

"Probably be a good idea."

She tipped back in the water, wishing... "I'd like to stay just a few more minutes, if you don't mind."

"No. I don't mind."

"All right." Mattie paddled around the pool a little, feeling a little awkward that he wasn't joining her.

He sat on a flat piece of pink granite at the edge of the pool and tossed pine needles at her.

After a little while, he asked, "Are you still mad at me?"

"No. You were right. I need to get this settled before I can move on." She swam a few strokes, reveling in the soft feeling of the water on her body. "I'll miss this place, though. It's like heaven."

He tossed a pine cone and it splashed in the water next to her. "You're welcome to come visit anytime."

Mattie looked at him.

His eyes were sober. "I mean it, Mattie. If I'm not here, you just go on in and make yourself at home."

She smiled ruefully, knowing she'd never take him up on the offer. "Thanks."

"You sure you don't want me to go with you?"

"I'm sure, Zeke. It's time I stood on my own two feet." To change the subject, she splashed water toward him. "Why don't you come in for a swim with me? Last chance."

He inclined his head. "I think I'd better wait out here."

Mattie shrugged, and kicked backward into a float. "Your loss."

She felt his gaze on her, hot and sharp, touching the curves exposed by the water—and she was glad. She hoped it was desperately hard for him to let her go.

"Mattie," he said. "About last night—"

She pulled herself upright. "Zeke, you said it best. It was great but it won't last, so let's just let it go. I can't stand to go through some mournful parting scene, okay?"

She could see that wounded him. His face went dark and he stood up. "Fine." He paced the side of the pool and glanced through the break in the trees. "I just thought it would be—"

He broke off, shoved his hand through his hair. "I don't know what I thought."

Mattie knew. "Let it go, Zeke," she said, suddenly weary. Wiping water from her face, she waded to shore. Picking up her towel, she echoed his words from the night before, "It was nice while it lasted, right?"

He didn't look at her, just stood at the break in the trees that looked down to the cabin, his jaw stern. "Yeah."

She looped the towel around her neck. "I'm going down."

"Mattie—"

The anguished sound had reached his voice now, thick and not entirely steady. Mattie closed her eyes, wondering what she should do, how she should handle this. Her heart ached for him, but if she offered herself, he would never really know what was in his heart. Nor would she.

But she waited, watching his face carefully. The pale green eyes were nearly emerald with boiling emotions and his face had never seemed harsher. He seemed about to speak.

But he just shook his head mutely.

Mattie headed down the hill.

It wasn't as easy to locate the turnoff as Brian had hoped. They stopped in three little towns, asking the same questions, over and over, with no success. Nobody knew Zeke Shephard.

By midmorning, the burn of frustration built again in Brian's chest, and Vince didn't make it any better, creeping along the mountain roads like a little old lady, his fingers white on the steering wheel. "Can't you go the speed limit?" Brian growled in frustration.

"Some of these cliffs have drops that are thousands of feet," Vince retorted. "You think you can do better, you drive."

Brian slumped impatiently.

Just before noon, they came to a small clearing on the road, featuring a fishing tackle shop and a gas station. Not even a café at this one, but they stopped all the same.

Brian shoved his fingers through his hair and got out. "Get some gas. I'll see if I can find anything out."

The old man behind the counter nodded as Brian came through the door. Brian picked out some candy bars—these old geezers always talked better if you were buying their merchandise—and sighed as he put them on the counter. How many times had he asked these questions? "I'm wondering if you can help me out here. My cousin has some land right around here somewhere. I'm supposed to be meeting him there to do some fishing, but I can't find the place. You know Zeke Shephard by any chance? He drives a blue motorcycle. Kinda big guy."

"Sure I know him!" The old man rang up the candy bars. "The horse breeder. You missed him by maybe forty-five minutes. He was just in here this morning, making a phone call."

Brian forced a friendly grin. "It figures. At least I'm close now. Can you tell me how to get there?"

The old man licked a thumb and counted out Brian's change. "Go on back the way you came, about five miles. There's a big split tree on one side, next to a pink boulder. Can't miss it. The road up to Zeke's place is about a hundred yards down the road on the other side.''

It wasn't exactly an address, but it was a hell of a lot closer than Brian had come yet. "Thanks."

Zeke paced the cabin restlessly, walking outside to the porch and back inside, listening. Mattie made some soup and he ate it mechanically, trying not to think about how he was going to feel when she climbed into that police car and rode out of his life. He didn't even know where she lived, how to reach her. The police would likely put her in a safe house, anyway. Out of reach of the crooks and bad guys, but out of Zeke's reach, as well. It made him feel a little panicky.

He finished the soup and went back to the porch to light a cigarette, staring out at the brightly lit view of the mountains. Inside, Mattie hummed as she cleared their dishes.

He walked to the end of the porch and stared down the road. A hollowness echoed in his chest and—
Damn.

"Mattie!" he called urgently, finally recognizing the warning signs. He'd been so preoccupied over her departure that he hadn't realized his instincts had been screaming for more than an hour. The hairs on the back of his neck prickled now and he called again. "Mattie!"

She came out to the porch, drying her hands on a small dish towel, her expression perplexed. "You don't have to yell. I'm right here."

Through the trees, Zeke caught sight of a flash of color, a yellow utterly at odds with the grays and blues of this landscape. He grabbed Mattie's arm roughly.

"I think we've got company." With a little shove, he directed her to the steps. "Go to the sauna and stay there no matter what you hear."

"Zeke, no! You can't—"

"Go." This time his shove was a little more insistent. "I can't be worrying about where you are right now. Get!"

She glared at him, but a snatch of a voice reached them through the trees and she jumped down the stairs.

Too late. Just as she landed in the small clearing, the two men Zeke had seen in the café broke through the trees. Both carried guns.

In that split second, standing too far from Mattie to do anything to help her, knowing she stood there because he'd called her outside, Zeke knew a splintering sense of despair.

Once again, the brutal forces of the world would triumph. Once again, he would prove himself unequal to them. Once again—

A vision of his father, smelling of sour beer, holding a cigarette to Zeke's thirteen-year-old side, sizzled through his mind, overlaying the scene with painful emotion. Rage, buried for twenty years, surfaced in a torrent. Rage deeper than the canyons, wider than the sky.

Zeke turned.

Reacting from the gut, from years and years of fighting a force bigger, stronger, meaner than himself, he let go of a rebel yell and launched himself, running at full speed toward the end of the porch. He vaulted over the railing and into the air. His legs, like the rest of him, were strong, and the leap hurtled him very close to Brian Murphy and his henchman.

Their attention had been on Mattie, frozen there in the clearing like a statue. Zeke landed and rolled, ducking his head in a classic football tackle, keeping low. His body caught Brian's at midthigh, and the man tumbled backward, gun flying. They went down together, rolling in a clinch down the hill.

Though not as big as Zeke, Brian was no small man, and he had muscle. The two of them came up fighting, and the struggle was mortal. Zeke held on to the wiry body, hurtling him backward into a tree, and felt the jarring through his own body, but Brian swung and caught Zeke clean on the mouth. A tooth gave way.

Zeke used his fists, his legs, every ounce of strength he'd gained in twenty years, fighting like it was his father and he had one more chance to put the past right. It lent him an unholy strength and gradually he gained the upper hand.

Mattie's scream brought him out of his furious trance. He let Brian go and bolted for the clearing, keeping his eyes open for the gun that had gone flying when he tackled Brian.

It gleamed dully in the grass and Zeke headed for it. He couldn't see Mattie anywhere, but heard her screams. Not fearful screams, but the kind to call attention. He could hear the slimy partner utter an epithet, clear in the mountain stillness, and Zeke knew Mattie was fighting, too.

Brian caught Zeke from behind, tackling him before he reached the gun, and the struggle began anew. Zeke landed a right to the jaw; Brian staggered and Zeke gained his feet.

Into the day broke the urgent sound of sirens. The sound distracted Brian long enough to allow Zeke to grab the gun and train it on his opponent's head. "Don't move."

He grabbed the back of the khaki Land's End jacket and hauled Brian to his feet, holding the gun at his head. Brian lifted his hands in classic surrender. "All right, man. All right. You win."

The sirens rang closer, and Zeke heard the sheriff's engine coming up the rutted track to the cabin, but he couldn't see Mattie. Couldn't see her or Vince. "Mattie!" he roared.

She emerged from the front door of the cabin, carrying her purse and tote. Vince held her by the collar, his gun held firmly at her back, and she stumbled a little. She looked scuffed, as if there had been a struggle.

Zeke scanned her face for signs of damage. Gone was the wide-eyed innocent, the fearful good girl. A smear of dust covered her chin and her hair was tousled, but it was her expression that changed her. Murderous.

"She's coming with me," Vince called out.

"Don't be stupid," Zeke returned. "How are you gonna get by the cops?" The sirens were nearly upon them.

"Big woods out there. We'll do it."

Brian jerked suddenly, as if to break free. Zeke grabbed a fistful of jacket and cocked the hammer of the gun. "I'd rather not shoot you, because it's too fast, but I will if I have to."

Vince pushed Mattie again, toward the trees on the side of the barn. She stumbled again, and Zeke wondered if he could get a clear shot at Vince if she ducked. The police wouldn't open fire on them. If he didn't do something, Vince would get away.

Simultaneously, he moved the gun, taking aim. The sheriff's white Jeep pulled into the clearing, siren screaming. Mattie fell to the ground and curled into a ball. Zeke had a clear shot, but abruptly, Vince dropped to the ground, too. Mattie had attacked his ankles and yanked his feet from beneath him. She was up and moving, but not fast enough. Vince scrambled to his feet.

Mattie turned, and he could hear the high, keening sound of her rage as she lifted that sturdy leather purse filled with rolls of quarters and smashed it into Vince's head. He went down.

Cold.

Zeke whooped and Mattie glanced over, breathing hard. Her mouth was split and she wiped at it, smearing blood into the mud on her chin. Calmly, she plucked the gun from Vince's hand and picked up her tote.

Next to Zeke, Brian was silent, watching Mattie approach. Red lights flashed and men were pouring from the two vehicles in the clearing, but Mattie ignored all of it. She walked with determination toward Zeke and Brian and stopped in front of them. From her purse, she pulled the three-foot braid she'd cut from her head and dropped it at Brian's feet.

Zeke stared at her, her breath coming hard, her thick straight hair scattered over her forehead, her eyes blazing. A high patch of color burned on each cheekbone. Her T-shirt had been torn a little at the neckline and gaped over her slim, beautiful shoulders.

Zeke wondered how the hell he'd ever thought her mild. And how the hell he was going to let her go.

Chapter 16

Brian and Vince were taken in one vehicle as the sheriff took Zeke and Mattie's statements.

Now everything had been done. Mattie stood outside the cabin with Zeke, her purse on her shoulder, the tote bag at her feet. The sheriff shook Zeke's hand. "I'll be in touch."

Zeke nodded.

The sheriff looked at Mattie. "Are you ready?"

She took a breath and nodded.

"Give us a minute, will you?" Zeke asked.

The man winked and nodded. "I'll wait in the Jeep."

A thin gray line of clouds showed to the west and Mattie eyed them for something to focus on so she would not break down and cry or something else equally stupid. "Looks like rain," she said, shifting her purse close.

"Yep." He touched her arm with one finger.

Mattie fidgeted with her strap, and finally looked at him. "Guess this is it."

His throat moved. "Guess it is." He took her hand. "Let me know how you are every now and then, okay? Call Roxanne at the café in Kismet, leave a message."

"Sure." She pressed her lips together, looked up at him. "Thank you for everything."

He nodded. "Remember, you're welcome anytime. Standing invitation."

She smiled. "Get your horse, Zeke. He loves you."

Something in his expression made her suspicious. "You are going to take the money, aren't you?"

He took a breath. "No. It's going to go into an account in your name in Kansas City. The sheriff will give you the number."

"Are you ever going to ask for anything for yourself, Zeke?"

He gestured toward the land. "I have what I need in this land, Miss Mary." He glanced at the Jeep and back to her. "You take care," he said, and stepped back.

Mattie inclined her head, for one long moment thinking of everything that had happened between them—from that first moment in the café to this moment—and she smiled again. "You're a good man, Zeke Shephard." Unafraid, she stepped forward and put her arms around his neck, standing on tiptoe to kiss his hard, sculpted cheek. "Be good."

His embrace was, for a fleeting instant, as fierce and sharp as a vise. "Take care, Miss Mary." He kissed her head. "Take care."

Then abruptly, Mattie was standing alone. He really was going to let her go. Carefully swallowing her emotions, she bent and grabbed her tote bag, and walked to the Jeep without a backward glance.

The next few weeks passed in a blur for Mattie. The Colorado State Patrol escorted her to Denver, where a Kansas City police officer waited to take her into the city. They took her statement and stowed her in a safe house. She didn't even have to insist that Brian was dangerous, that he had connections and wouldn't rest until Mattie was dead. The small victory at Zeke's cabin had only been a minor skirmish in the battle— satisfactory but hardly conclusive. The police weren't going to take any chances that their sole witness might meet an accident.

She had a friend check her apartment. Mattie's collection of library books had been boxed carefully by the manager, who'd known how Mattie valued the books, and put in storage. Her job, of course, had been filled.

The days dragged. Mattie hated being back in the city. Everything she'd learned to love about the outdoors seemed perverted here. She had grown used to silence, and the constant flow of noise in the city made her irritable. Car horns and telephones and people talking; televisions, radios, refrigerators humming. Everywhere she went, there was noise.

Her nose had grown sensitive to the subtle scents of pine and water and a man's skin. Exhaust fumes and stale smoke and blacktop permeated the air here.

The worst, though, was the heat and humidity. In the mountains, she'd grown used to the light, sweet air. Here the air seemed to strangle her and the heat weighed on her body like an iron.

The bad-temperedness was partly by choice, of course. Mattie knew that. She didn't want to be here. Kansas City had been her home all of her life, but she'd only found herself when she left it. Now she felt a prisoner to a life that wasn't her own anymore.

She tried not to think about Zeke. Long ago she'd learned to be pragmatic about life: she accepted what she couldn't change. Zeke fell into that category, but she caught herself more than once sitting by a window, willing him to come striding up the walk.

She missed him painfully. It seemed impossible that she could have formed a deeper connection with a man she'd known three weeks than with people she'd known most of her adult life. But she had.

There was nothing she could do about that, either.

Because Brian was a cop-killer, because the Kansas City police had been looking for a break in their attempt to put him away for several years, there wasn't a long wait for the trial. On a late summer morning, hot and humid, Mattie dressed carefully, brushed her newly trimmed hair, and promptly threw up her breakfast.

Standing in the air-conditioned bathroom, painted pale blue, Mattie stared at herself in the mirror. Was she still so afraid? How could he possibly hurt her?

The person who stared back was hardly the same meek, mild woman who'd never stood up for herself, who settled for the ugly coat and let promotions pass her by. This woman was strong and her face showed it. There was a tilt to her chin. Her eyes were clear and direct. A healthy glow lit her cheeks.

No, she wasn't afraid. A strong man, a good man, had loved her and brought her to life. Nothing could change that. Nothing could ever take it away.

Zeke sat on his back porch and played tug-of-war with a sloppy, shaggy ball of loose black fur and tiny sharp teeth. "You call yourself a dog?" he said, shaking the rag the puppy clutched between his teeth. "Come on, let me see some real teeth."

The Labrador growled happily, then let loose of the rag and dived for Zeke's hand, sloppily licking it and rolling over to have his tummy rubbed. Zeke chuckled and scooped him up, cuddling him in the crook of an arm to rub his head and body. "Can't be doing this forever, Tommyboy," he said with affection. "You'll be too big and then you'll want to be a lapdog."

The puppy heaved a sigh of contentment.

Zeke sighed, too. He hadn't owned a dog since childhood, but the days and night just after Mattie left had been almost unbearably lonely. One morning, he'd gone to town with nothing in mind but finding a puppy to keep him company. Surprised even Zeke how much it helped. Tommy followed him around everywhere he went, provided someone to talk to during meals, even slept in his bed at night, a warm, breathing comfort in the dark and lonely nights.

For most of the summer, he'd felt suspended, as if he were waiting for something he couldn't quite name. He'd managed to save a little cash, but sooner or later he'd have to find something to do to tide him over, or get moving somewhere for the winter.

He called Kismet twice to see if Mattie had left him any messages. The first time, she'd called to let him know she was safe, and that the trial was set. The second time, there was no message, and Roxanne chided him gently. "You want to leave one for her?"

Zeke said, "Just tell her the invitation stands."

"You are the stubbornest man," Roxanne replied. "Even over five hundred miles, I can tell you're as lovesick as you can be. Why don't you just admit it?"

"You're imagining things as usual, Roxie," he said and hung up.

But as he sat in the smoky dusk of a summer evening, with a puppy curled in his arms, Zeke had to admit he missed Mattie with something close to desperation.

She was the only woman he'd ever been himself with completely; somehow, she'd made him free to be. She'd freed him from his prison of self-pity and despair, too, with a simple, wide-open enjoyment of life. Mattie made him remember he was somebody, that he had things to give.

An engine on the road made him jump to his feet, his heart leaping with hope. Maybe she'd taken him up on his invitation, after all. Maybe she'd come back for a short visit and—

The truck belonged to George Romero. He was pulling a horse trailer, and the bed of the pickup was filled with hay. "Hey, neighbor," Zeke called, trying to quell his disappointment. "What brings you my way?"

George leaped nimbly from the cab, grinning. "What you got there? One of Lowry's pups, eh? I got one, too." He tickled the puppy under the chin and let himself be licked. "Damn good dogs, but you don't have any sheep."

"Neither do you."

"Wool's on the upswing these days. I may think about it."

Zeke nodded. "You didn't come all the way up here to talk about wool and dogs."

"Nope." He walked to the foot of the horse trailer and led out Othello. "I brought you back your damned, mean horse."

Zeke frowned. "I don't get it."

"That woman of yours paid for him by certified check, yesterday."

"Mattie?" A swell of hope burst into his chest. "Is she here?"

George shook his head, giving Zeke the lead rope. Othello lifted his head and snuffled happily at Zeke and the puppy. "Nah, she mailed it from Kansas City."

"Hey, buddy," Zeke said quietly. He didn't look at George for fear his disappointment would be too obvious.

"She told me to tell you that this was not for you, it was for your horse." He chuckled. "She has some pride, that one."

"Yeah."

"How long you gonna wait?"

Zeke looked up. "For what?"

"To go after her. I'll come feed this monster. We've kinda gotten used to each other."

"Thanks for the offer, but I'm not going after her. She knows where I am if she wants to live this kind of life."

George snorted. "You're a real easy man to approach, too, aren't you, Zeke?"

"What's that supposed to mean?"

"You've got 'no trespassing' written on every bone of your body. If you want that woman, you'll have to go get her."

"She knows where I am," he repeated stubbornly. But for one minute, he wished he were another sort of man, one that could give Mattie that home and family she wanted so much. But she knew his terms—no commitments and no children. And he didn't think she'd go for it.

It wasn't until the trial was over that she admitted to herself that she'd really expected Zeke to show up. It had taken two weeks, but the jury deliberated exactly one hour before returning with a guilty verdict. Brian Murphy would be in prison a long, long time.

As she walked into her small apartment bedroom, finally free, Mattie at last admitted Zeke wasn't going to come after her.

It was painful to admit she'd been hoping just that all these weeks. His expression that last day, that loneliness and need she'd seen at the pool, had given her hope.

She brushed sticky hair back from her sticky forehead. He'd told her it would be this way. She just hadn't accepted it.

With a sigh, she began to collect her things. At least she'd been able to arrange to have Othello returned to him, so he wouldn't be so utterly alone. Maybe that was all she could do for him.

It was time to face facts and make choices.

One thing was clear: she would not stay in Kansas City. Thanks to Zeke's unselfishness, she had a fat, healthy bank account, money that gave her more freedom than she'd ever dreamed could exist. Not only could she leave Kansas City forever, she was free to choose any place in the world she wanted to live, and go there.

Colorado or Arizona?

Packing her thin, worn tank top and shorts, she grinned wryly. They really were ugly. Maybe something else she should do was buy some new clothes. Her bra pinched her when she bent, and she shifted it back into place, wincing a little at the tenderness of her breasts. None of her bras fit right at the moment and—

Her heart started pounding. Holding a pair of jeans in her hands, she sank down on the bed, trying to remember how long it had been since she'd dropped that blasted box of tampons in front of Zeke at her cabin in Kismet.

Almost three months.

Breathlessly, she tried to calm her racing thoughts, so she could think clearly. She'd often been irregular in her cycle when she was younger, and had attributed this irregularity to stress and change in her life. But three months was a long time. And sore breasts. And the nausea before the trial. And her sleepiness.

Sitting there with her clothes scattered all around her, her life in total upheaval, Mattie bent her head and touched her belly. A baby.

A baby.

Forever and ever she'd wanted her own family, people to love and care for. She'd imagined a whole family unit, mother and father and child, with animals and messes and chaos.

A baby.

She remembered each time she'd made love to Zeke and wondered which one had resulted in this child.

The wild moment in the shower? The tender times through the night?

Joy welled up inside her, cutting through surprise and dismay with a blazing, cleansing light. A baby. It didn't matter that the details were not exactly what she'd hoped or that the union that produced the child had not been blessed by the Holy Church.

She was going to have a child, Zeke's child.

That changed everything.

Snow came early to the southern Rockies, and this year was no exception. The first snow began to fall just past the middle of September. Zeke was prepared with hay for the horses, plenty of food for himself, the truck serviced and gassed up. Stacks of wood were piled by the cabin and the sauna.

In the snowy dusk, he went out to feed the horses. Othello whinnied in greeting, head tossing in cheerful acknowledgement of the flakes drifting down in sparkling wonder. Nearby, calmly watching the landscape, was a new Appaloosa mare. Zeke had sold his motorcycle and used part of the money to put a down payment on a loan to buy her.

The rest of the loan he'd used for a very practical purpose—he hired an electrician to wire the cabin, and he'd added a room at the back of the house, with views of the mountains. It was a little strange to be able to flip a switch and have a light come on, but he was getting used to it. He had to admit it was nice to have a refrigerator again.

The work had kept him distracted somewhat. Now he had to face a long, gaping winter with nothing to fill it. Weren't many projects a man could tackle in the mountains in the winter.

He'd called Kismet again last week. Not a word from Mattie since the last time he'd called, when she reported Brian was safely in prison.

As he shoveled the stalls, he gave himself a talk. Maybe George and Roxanne were right. What was he gaining by cloaking himself in stubborn pride? He missed the woman with a relentless, aching pain that never went away. His first thought in the morning was Mattie. He drifted off to sleep thinking of her. At night, his dreams were filled with the feeling of her, all around him.

After all those years and all those women, Zeke was in love. It was a lot harder than he thought it would be. A much bigger problem than he'd expected. He couldn't shove it under a carpet in his mind and let it go away. Not that he didn't try.

It just kept crawling out. He'd be playing with Tommy and wonder how Mattie felt about dogs. He rode through the mountains, on his own land on his own horse, and wanted to teach her how to ride. The gentle mare was made for a small woman like Mattie, and Zeke hadn't given the animal a name.

He sighed and shook his head. He didn't want to go through this winter without her. He didn't want another day to pass without seeing her again. If he didn't at least try, he'd be lost the rest of his life.

In the corrals beyond the barn, the horses whinnied. Tommy, who'd been happily snuffling through the stables, jumped up and started barking urgently. The puppy rushed to the doors.

Curious over who in the world would have made the trek up here in this kind of weather, he propped his shovel against the wall, brushed off his jeans and ambled out.

Mattie.

Chapter 17

His heart slammed to a stop. As the blood stilled in his body, he stared at her, wondering with a blank sense of unreality if his longing had conjured her up.

She stood uncertainly by the fence, wearing a pretty coat of purple and green with gold in a brocade pattern all over it, and jeans. And a good pair of Zodiac boots with low heels. Her hair gleamed in the pinkish light, and fat clumps of snow stuck to it.

"I hope you meant it," she said at last. "I took you up on your invitation."

The blood in his body unfroze, and rushed through him in a blistering wash. He didn't move, afraid if he did, he'd overwhelm her. "I'm glad."

Slowly, he crossed the space between them, feeling as if he couldn't breathe properly. Close to her, he stopped. "You mind if I give you a welcome hug?"

The wide brown eyes flickered. "No," she said softly. "Not at all."

Zeke bent and wrapped his arms around her. She flowed into his embrace as if she were pieces lost from him, and he held her close, so close, breathing in the smell of her hair, the feel of her small, rounded body, the feel of her hair against his cheek. He closed his eyes, almost dizzy with the reality of her, now, next to him. "It hasn't been the same without you, Miss Mary."

Once he had her, he didn't want to let go, and they stood there, rocking slowly together in the falling snow, until Tommy got jealous and jumped on their legs. He yapped and made a soft whine.

Mattie chuckled and eased away. "Who is this?" She knelt, smiling, to rub the puppy's head.

"Tommy."

"What a cutie," she said in a sweet dog-voice. Tommy fell instantly in love, and jumped up to lick her face.

Zeke knew just how he felt. "You want to go in and have some coffee?" he asked, trying to remember to be civilized.

"Sure." She stuck her hands in her pockets. "I hope this isn't a bad time or anything. I didn't have any way to call and warn you."

"No time would be a bad time," he said. "I'm glad you're here."

She smiled, but there was something hesitant still. He didn't want to acknowledge anything uneven just yet, though. It was enough to just have her here. "I have a surprise for you. Come on."

Mattie followed him in, and the smile on her face was worth the hassles of the wiring when he flipped the switch and a lamp at the table side came on. "Ta-da," he said with a flourish, gesturing. "Lamps. Radio—"

He flipped it on, and just as quickly off when the sound intruded. "Even a fridge. So you can have real milk in your coffee."

She laughed. "I'm amazed you could get so much done so fast."

Fast. It seemed like a hundred years since he'd seen her last. A thousand. "Let me take your coat."

Admiring the new appliances, she absently took it off and looked up to give it to him, her eyes shining. Below the coat, she wore a soft, gauzy blouse with long, romantic sleeves and a scoop neck. Her waist was accentuated with a belt made of silver conchos, and swinging from her ears were silver feathers. He lifted an eyebrow. "You got you some new clothes."

"Yes, I did." She grinned. "Do you like them?"

"Look like you were born and raised in the West."

She smoothed her palms on her jeans. "Thanks. The amazing thing is, I have more than just these. A whole closetful of clothes."

The silky fabric of her blouse clung to her breasts with a loving hand. The jeans hugged her generous hips. "Puts a man in mind of things other than coffee," he said, and was amazed to hear his voice was hoarse.

"Does it?" she said in a near whisper.

"I'd sure like to kiss you."

"I wouldn't mind," she said, and swallowed.

He tossed her coat on the chair and moved swiftly to take her face in his hands and press his mouth to hers. Her hands fell on his wrists, and when their lips met, she made a tiny little sound, almost pained.

He got dizzy. Dizzy as if he'd been on a merry-go-round for ten minutes, so dizzy he nearly swayed. And it made him dip again, taste her gently, sweetly. "Oh,

Mattie," he sighed and pulled her close to kiss her properly. "I missed you so much."

It seemed right, natural, to lead her into the new bedroom, with its wide views of the mountains, now obscured with falling snow. A room he'd built with her in mind, a room with thick braided rugs on the floor and a nice lamp.

But he trembled as he unbuttoned her blouse, for there was too much inside of him. Too much. He skimmed off her blouse and touched her breasts and waist, kissed one pert nipple as gently as he could. And pulled her close again, feeling her nakedness against him.

"I love you, Mattie," he whispered against her ear.

The words released something, and he said it again. "I love you."

"Zeke," she said in a strangled voice, her fingers clutching his body. He felt a wash of moisture on her face and lifted her chin to kiss the tears.

"I love you," he whispered, and lifted her gently in his arms. They made love slowly, with a savoring hunger born of weeks of longing. He took the time to kiss the round of her shoulder and the crook of her arm, the gentle rise of her belly and the curve of a thigh.

Even their climax seemed calm and full and deep, rocking and rippling, not wild or fierce. As they lay together sated, Mattie said, "I love you."

He braced himself on his arms and kissed her, his hair falling around their faces like a curtain. "Will you stay?"

She hesitated. "We need to talk, Zeke."

The tone of her voice sent a bolt of fear through him, but he didn't want to give this up yet, this feeling of being whole; of the world, for one brief instant, being right. "Not yet, Mattie. Let me just love you."

"It's really important."

This time, real alarm sounded and he moved away, erecting defenses against whatever it was. In the instant it took to separate himself, put some space between them, he tried to imagine what could put that tone in her voice. Another man? Some glitch with the trial? A sudden desire to travel and see the world?

Her face gave no reassurance, either. She pulled the covers up around her, and her eyes were big with worry.

"Damn, Mattie, just tell me."

She swallowed, brushed her hair off her forehead and said, "I'm going to have a baby."

He gaped at her, not comprehending. Had she been carrying Brian's child when he met her? No. He remembered that box of tampons she spilled. "A baby?"

She licked her lips. "Yes. I wasn't going to tell you, because you made your position very clear. And I'm not asking anything of you, either."

Zeke heard a roaring in his ears. "*My* child?"

"I didn't think it was fair to not tell you. I kept thinking of the way you looked with that baby in the bar in Kismet, and it just seemed wrong not to tell you."

He felt as if he'd had the wind knocked out of him. Urgently, he stood up and grabbed his robe. He tied it firmly. "You're pregnant?"

"Yes."

"Oh, Mattie," he said, and sank into a chair, covering his face. "A baby."

"I'm sorry, Zeke." She grabbed her clothes from the floor where they had fallen and started yanking them on. "I shouldn't have come. I'm sorry. It seemed like the right thing to do."

He looked up, startled. "What are you doing?"

"I'll just go, um, back to my place. I'm living in town."

He jumped up, one fear overriding the other. If she left again, he'd face all that bleak loneliness again. "No," he said, grabbing her. "No." He pulled her into his arms, holding her so she couldn't go. "Don't leave me again, Mattie. Please."

"Oh, Zeke," she said, flinging her arms around his neck. She burst into tears. "I never wanted to leave in the first place."

He closed his eyes and held her close. "Don't go," he repeated in a whisper.

"No, Zeke. I won't." She held him. "I won't."

They sat by the fire in the living room, drinking hot chocolate and eating popcorn. Zeke held her as if he wasn't sure he wanted to let go, and Mattie stayed close for the same reason. It seemed like a miracle.

After a time, he said quietly, "It scares me, Mattie, the baby."

She lifted her head. "I know."

"It's been the one thing I most regretted, that I wasn't gonna have any babies of my own." His drawl seemed deeper, as it always did when references to his childhood emerged. "What if I'm like him, Mattie? What if that meanness is living in me somewhere?"

Mattie looked at him for a long moment, thinking of all the reasons she knew he wasn't mean, not anywhere in him, not the tiniest portion. "This is a gift,

Zeke, from heaven above. If a star fell in your lap, would you give it back to God and tell him you didn't think you could handle it?"

He stroked her hair. "No"

"You know what I think?" Mattie said, and touched his face. "I think you're my reward for making it through. I think this baby is your reward for being so brave all those years." She touched one of the small faded circle scars. "I think you deserve to have a baby of your own more than anyone I've ever met."

He yanked her close, burying his head against her neck, but not before Mattie saw the glimmer of tears in his eyes. "You're my reward, Miss Mary."

In time, when he'd gained control, he lifted his head. "So you think you want to live with a man like me, huh? Up here in the wilderness without a toilet and no movie house for thirty miles?"

"Yes."

"You think you're going to enjoy a life of raising horses?"

"Yes."

He took a breath. "And you think you want me to be the father of your children?"

She lifted her head, smiling. "Definitely."

He nodded. "I think we oughta get married, then, don't you?"

"Yes."

"We do have one small problem, Miss Mary," he said in his gravelly voice.

"What?"

"You never told me your name. Is Mattie really short for Matilda?"

She laughed. "Will it change things?"

"It might. I don't know about being married to Matilda."

"Look who's talking, *Ezekiel*."

"So it *is* Matilda." He chuckled.

"It's Madeline."

He went still. "Really?"

"Rhetta Madeline O'Neal. Irish as they come."

"Madeline was my sister's name," he said hoarsely, pressing his lips to her temple. "The one who died."

Mattie leaned into him, pressing her cheek to his neck.

"If the baby is a girl, maybe we could call her Madeline, if you wouldn't mind."

Mattie didn't bother to stop the tears. "That would be fine."

He stroked her arm gently. "And what was your foster brother's name? The one who taught you to play pool?"

"Jamie," she whispered, hearing his acceptance of the child they'd made.

"That would be nice for a boy."

"Very nice," she agreed and let him gather her up close.

Silent, contented, they watched the fire flicker as snow fell from a peaceful mountain sky.

* * * * *

Dark secrets, dangerous desire...

Lovers DARK AND DANGEROUS

Three spine-tingling tales from the dark side
of love.

This October, enter the world of shadowy
romance as Silhouette presents the third in their
annual tradition of thrilling love stories and
chilling story lines. Written by three of
Silhouette's top names:

LINDSAY McKENNA
LEE KARR
RACHEL LEE

Haunting a store near you this October.

HE'S AN

AMERICAN HERO

Men of mettle. Men of integrity. Real men who know the real meaning of love. Each month, Intimate Moments salutes these true American Heroes.

For July: THAT SAME OLD FEELING,
by Judith Duncan.
Chase McCall had come home a new man. Yet old lover Devon Manyfeathers soon stirred familiar feelings—and renewed desire.

For August: MICHAEL'S GIFT,
by Marilyn Pappano.
Michael Bennett knew his visions prophesied certain death. Yet he would move the high heavens to change beautiful Valery Navarre's fate.

For September: DEFENDER,
by Kathleen Eagle.
Gideon Defender had reformed his bad-boy ways to become a leader among his people. Yet one habit—loving Raina McKenny—had never died, especially after Gideon learned she'd returned home.

AMERICAN HEROES: Men who give all they've got for their country, their work—the women they love.

Only from

INTIMATE MOMENTS®
Silhouette®

You've met Gable, Cooper and Flynn Rawlings.
Now meet their spirited sister, Kat Rawlings, in
her own installment of

THE WILD WEST

by Linda Turner

Kat admitted it—she was once a spoiled brat.
But these days she focused all her attention
on making her ranch successful. Until
Lucas Valentine signed on as her ranchhand.
Sexy as hell, the bitter cast to his smile pointed to
a past that intrigued her. The only problem was
that Lucas seemed bent on ignoring the sparks
between them. Yet Kat *always* got what she
wanted—and she was readying her lasso,
because her heart was set on Lucas!

Don't miss KAT (IM #590), the exciting
conclusion to Linda Turner's Wild West saga.
Available in September, only from
Silhouette Intimate Moments!

**And now Silhouette offers you
something completely different....**

SPELLBOUND
R O M A N C E

**In September, look for
SOMEWHERE IN TIME (IM #593)
by Merline Lovelace**

Commander Lucius Antonius was intrigued
by his newest prisoner. Although spirited
Aurora Durant didn't behave like any woman
he knew, he found her captivating. But why did
she wear such strange clothing, speak Rome's
language so haltingly and claim to fly in a silver
chariot? Lucius needed to uncover *all* Aurora's
secrets—including what "an air force pilot lost
in time" meant—before he succumbed to her
tempting lures and lost his head, as well as
his heart....